INTOXICATION

Intoxication

Cathryn Cooper

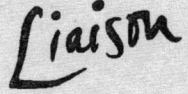

First published in 1998
by HEADLINE BOOK PUBLISHING

10 9 8 7 6 5 4 3 2 1

ISBN 0 7472 5820 1

Typeset by CBS, Felixstowe, Suffolk

Printed and bound in Great Britain by
Mackays of Chatham plc, Chatham, Kent

HEADLINE BOOK PUBLISHING
A division of Hodder Headline PLC
338 Euston Road
London NW1 3BH

Intoxication

Chapter 1

'Was that good for you, Gloria?'

Gloria sighed. Her whole body seemed to shiver, her muscles rippling beneath her skin as his hand swept down over her back. Spreading his fingers wide, he held both buttocks as if he were holding a pair of plump, ripe watermelons. He squeezed.

'Ooow, Bluey baby!' Gloria purred like a satisfied feline, arching her back so that her naked belly touched his and her nipples brushed the hairs of his chest.

'It was divine.' She pursed lips that had once been plush with scarlet lipstick. They were now their natural pink, the colour sucked and kissed away by his mouth. Her bottle-blonde hair fell in spring-like curls, peek-a-boo fashion, over her baby-blue eyes. Everything about her was designed to tempt, to be pleasing to the eye. Gloria was like an iced cake decorated with brightly blushing roses or sparkling spangles. But beneath the icing it was easy to see that she was as simple as a sponge, devoid of the richness of thought that might have made her interesting.

But Blue didn't care that her mind was full of air. He hardly noticed what she said, and anyway, what she said apleased him. She praised his looks, praised his sexual prowess, and at this moment in time, it was all he cared about.

'Good enough for you to let me do it again?' His voice was husky against her hair.

'My, my, Blue! Could you really do it again? I mean – that quick?' Gloria's voice was full of breathless excitement.

'Try it out. Feel me.'

Holding her gaze with his own, he took hold of her hand and guided it to the shadowed space between their bodies.

'Oooow!' Gloria gasped as her fingers touched his velvet-gloved erection. 'Wow! Big already? What a man you are, Blue Bonecci! What a man!'

He sighed and half closed his eyes as the thrill of her touch went through him. 'Only one of me, baby!'

Gloria murmured with delight as he ran his hand down to her knee and lifted her leg high and wide.

'You mustn't do that!'

She wriggled her toes and struggled a little as if she really meant it.

'Of course I must.' He held her ankle tight, his hair falling limp and damp over his forehead as he feasted his eyes on her open sex.

A pink blush washed over Gloria's face. She turned her head into the pillow as if unwilling to face her own shame or the look of sheer lust in her lover's eyes.

Wedging her ankle on his shoulder so that her toes tangled in his hair, Blue mounted her without any need to guide his stiff muscle into her wide open gateway.

'Oh no! You mustn't.' Gloria's protests melted to muted

groans of submission. His stomach slapped against hers. His pubic hair tangled and rasped against her own. His buttocks hollowed each time he withdrew then plunged himself back into her.

'How's that for you now, pretty baby?' he growled.

Gloria moaned something low and unintelligible, but gasped as he took hold of her other leg, his fingers leaving red marks against the whiteness of her inner thigh as he wedged her left ankle on his shoulder.

Gloria howled, her cries an odd mix of pain and pleasure, unable to form real words as the sensual sensations gripped her.

The sound of their breathing filled the room, along with a gentle slapping sound. Like ripples on a lake; like the sound of a fly screen door bumping against dry wood.

His balls, thought Una as she watched the pair of them make love. She had often savoured the sound of his balls as they had slapped against *her* bare flesh in those moments when *she* had been the woman in bed with him.

Her heart thudded in her chest as if her rib cage were small, too bird-like to contain it. She could have run from her hiding place, but the power of her feelings froze her to the spot. Through the criss-crossed lattice work of a bamboo screen, she watched the man she loved lying with a woman she despised.

Her breasts trembled with half-smothered sobs as she watched his body thud against that of the groaning Gloria. She could see his balls swinging, a dark heaviness between his thighs that she would have liked to finger or kiss. She'd done that before; kissed his hanging balls, relishing the touch of the soft down against her lips, the smell of recent male sweat, and the gentle curve of his buttocks before her eyes.

There was a dryness in her throat and she tried desperately to swallow each time Blue clenched his buttocks and heaved himself away from Gloria before lunging into her again. When he did that, she saw the base and first few inches of his stem and knew he was stiff; knew that she was forgotten and he was revelling in the woman beneath him.

Cheeks burning, Una blinked away angry tears. Narrowing her eyes, she attempted to look away, but found it impossible. Even though her sight was impaired by the moisture that flowed from her eyes, she had to watch. She loved his body even though it wasn't her he was loving tonight.

From memory she knew his skin would be warm to the touch and slightly moist. The memory cut her so deeply, she grabbed at her stomach because she felt real pain; felt as if she was bleeding inside.

Longing to scream, but not daring to utter a sound, she clenched her fists and bit her lip.

Stop it! This isn't like you! The words seared through Una's mind like an angry flame. *Don't let it hurt. Don't turn yourself into a martyr.*

She blinked away the tears and set her jaw firm and square. Never before had she let a man get to her like this. She hated Blue for it and a new kind of ache settled somewhere beneath her heart. She wanted revenge and she aimed to get it. But she would need help from others he had treated badly. God knew, there were plenty of those.

Chapter 2

'He's late.'

The voice seemed to echo around the oak-panelled room, the bookshelves and the comfortable, but masculine, leather armchairs and sofas.

A reclining nude, buttocks pink and dimpled, ankles crossed, smiled demurely down at them from the gilt-framed painting above the black marble fireplace. Cigar smoke from a rich Havana curled up like a scrap of muslin in front of her overblown nudity, but did not veil it.

Along with the cigar smoke, an air of expectancy hung in the room and, for a while, so did silence.

Three pairs of eyes glanced momentarily at the man who had spoken before they looked away, their expressions betraying nothing of what they were thinking.

'Chasing pussy again, knowing my brother.'

No one even looked up this time. The speaker chuckled nervously. The sobriety of the room remained unaltered. Everything was still and silent, except for the odd creak of leather as a backside was shifted in a seat and the insistent ticking of a grandfather clock.

As if only recently aware of its presence, the man who

had spoken – the youngest in the room – got up, walked round his chair and stood face to face with the clock. He glanced up at it as he pulled a pocket watch from the dark blue vest he was wearing. Squinting slightly, he glanced down at his watch, then peered into the porcelain face of the larger timepiece, which had brass hands and paintings of swans at each corner.

'They call these things grandfather clocks,' he pronounced, 'but you know, they're really called long case clocks. Made in England originally.'

Looks of subdued surprise were exchanged among his comrades.

'And how would you know something like that, Tony,' said Aldo Verecchia, a man with little hair, but a wide, thick-lipped mouth beneath a coarse-haired moustache. 'You've only just learned how to tie your shoe laces.'

Tony's jaw clenched as he feasted his eyes on the four swans that swam on four blue ponds in each corner of the clock face. He stared hard at them as if willing them to fly away.

'Yeah, but I wouldn't do it in your company, Verecchia. Not with my butt turned in your direction anyway!' There was mockery in his voice.

'Why you . . . !' Verecchia sprang from his chair, spun the younger man round, and gripped his collar and tie in hands as broad as shovels. 'If you weren't Blue's brother, I'd . . .'

A restraining hand came between them. A voice spoke slowly, calmly – almost coldly.

'But he *is* Blue's brother, Verecchia. Leave it be.'

Verecchia's face came close to Tony's. 'He's too pretty to be true, and he might have to watch his butt yet!' Spittle sprayed the younger man's face.

Tony blinked, but there was fire in his eyes, not fear.

'Sit down. Both of you.'

The heat in both men died to a simmer as Ice, the third man, eased them firmly but gently apart.

'Let's sit.' The third man's voice was neither loud nor demanding. It had an irresistible quality about it that inspired immediate response in the same way as a switch-blade knife. Ice was never ruffled. His thoughts were always concise, just like his voice and his actions. Unlike his nickname, he never showed any sign of melting.

Ice had grey eyes and short, silvery hair. His face was sharp, his frame lean, shoulders angular, and he towered a good six inches above the other two.

'This waiting gets to you, Ice,' said the fourth man who until now had merely watched in the same way that a spectator watches a boxing match; at a distance, but always in comfort. He was leaning forward in his chair, elbows resting on knees. 'Or at least,' he went on, 'the waiting gets to them.' He nodded at Verecchia and Tony.

'Especially waiting in silence,' added Tony. He glared at the other two, but not up at Ice whose height continued to dominate.

Ice lay his hand on Tony's shoulder and pressed him gently but firmly into his chair. 'Then let's talk.'

Verecchia grunted some sort of agreement as he sat down, then covered half his face with his hand and stared at his crossed ankles and the brown and white shoes beyond the

7

flashy checks of his brown and white suit.

The fourth man – nicknamed the Professor – a man as dapper as a weasel, took a deep breath.

'To talk, we need to have a subject in common and we each know something about it that the others do not know.'

The other three looked at him blankly. Ice was the first to speak.

'What do you mean, Prof?'

The man addressed as Prof adjusted the wire-framed glasses that perched precariously on the bridge of his nose. Behind their lenses, his quick eyes flickered as he spoke.

'Good conversation should use a subject that each of us knows about, but each have our own experience of. Experience, you see, is individual.'

Only Ice nodded.

'You mean like we've all experienced sex, so we've all got our own angles on that. And us all knowing Blue, but all having different experiences of him, would be of interest to everyone else. Sound about right?'

Prof nodded. 'Yes. That is exactly right.' He turned to Tony. 'Like Tony here is his brother, so he's bound to know more about Blue than we do – at least – from his early years. Is that not right, Tony?'

Tony had been frowning, but the Prof had asked for his opinion. A sudden sense of importance lightened his features. 'You want me to tell you stuff I know about him?'

Verecchia grumbled a kind of laugh behind his hand.

Unsmiling, Ice threw Verecchia a warning look before addressing Blue's brother. 'That's what I mean, kid.'

'A few anecdotes to pass the time,' Prof added. 'Some of

the things that happened to Blue when he was a boy.' The Prof laughed. 'Including a few stories about his sex life. They should be pretty entertaining.'

Tony laughed too. He shook his head as he began to remember. 'Oh boy. Do I know some things about sex. And do I know some things about my brother.'

Ice settled himself against a roll top desk and folded his arms. His steel grey eyes settled grimly upon Tony Bonecci. Tony gave no sign of having noticed the hint of contempt in the look. Why should he? His brother was a powerful man in the boot-legging trade. 'Then tell us what your brother was like when he was growing up.' His voice was as cold as his name.

Tony rested his hands on the chair arms and settled his head comfortably against the back of the smooth leather.

'My brother, the sex machine!' Tony laughed.

The others merely smiled or stared expectantly. Tony did not notice the deeper emotions in each man's eyes. But if he had done, he might have judged that they knew something he did not.

Chapter 3

'Lucy Lovit we used to call her, and no prizes for why we gave her that name,' Tony began, grinning broadly. 'She'd saunter on by, swinging her handbag on one finger, and chewing gum. I remember that her lips were always bright red but smudged; as if she'd been sucking on cherries or something.' He grinned, raised his eyebrows and shook his head. 'It certainly wasn't that kind of fruit she'd been sucking on. That babe was into sucking other things, and just looking at her advertised the fact. Her hair was Harlow blonde, crimped in waves around her face – a bit like that dame Gloria that's been hanging around my brother lately.'

The others exchanged swift glances. Tony was too lost in his reminiscences to notice.

'Summer or winter, she always wore a fox fur around her neck. Thought it gave her a look of class, I guess. I remember thinking that the eyes of the dead fox didn't glint as much as hers did. Both had green eyes. Hers were outlined with stacks of make-up. If you had a mind, you could tell the weather by that make-up. It drizzled down her face when it rained.

'We kids used to call her names; walk behind her wiggling our rears like she did. Not that she ever paid much attention to us, mind. Not until Blue was about eighteen and looked at her in as sassy a way as she looked at him.

'At eighteen, Blue wasn't that much different to look at than he is now. He was young but built like a man. Back then, his hair was as uncontrollable as it is now. It used to fall over his eyes and he used to toss his head so he could see straight. The dames used to love that. Still do.

'Anyway, Lucy Lovit noticed my brother and she took to smiling directly at him as she sashayed by. And that sashay got more and more . . .'

Tony ceased talking as he outlined the shape of a woman's hips with his hands, then waved them from side to side in an attempt to describe how Lucy Lovit had moved.

'We get the picture,' said Ice. 'Go on.'

Tony licked his lips. 'We used to crowd in a dark alley at the side of Mo Marks's Delicatessen – about four of us.' He grinned and blushed slightly as the memory came back to him. 'We used to compare what we had. You know?'

The others nodded as they remembered their own boyish curiosity about other boys' tackle.

'I remember.' Verecchia smiled suggestively, but stopped once Ice had fixed him with a hard, grey stare. Tony carried on.

'All of us each held our cocks in our hands and we were wanking like mad, of us racing to see who could bring it off first. I was almost there before I realised that Blue had stopped. His cock was still in his hand and still stiff and I remember wishing I had one as big as he did. But Blue's interest was elsewhere. I looked to where he was looking. And there she was, Lucy Lovit was standing there, her eyes as big as plates and her mouth open.

'"You aiming to waste that honey?" she asked. Her mouth hung wide enough to take a baseball, and her tongue licked along her lower lip as if my brother's cock was the biggest and best salami she had ever set eyes on.

'Blue being Blue didn't stay silent for long. I remember him grinning, and in that moment, I knew what he had in mind. Just thinking about it was enough to make me come in my hand. But I didn't.

'"What you want to do with it?" Blue asked her.

'I remember her smiling as she stepped forward. She licked her lips as she smiled. Never seemed to stop licking them. I wondered if she'd have dribbled if she hadn't – you know – like dogs do when they're about to get their dinner? Her eyes were looking into ours, but also looking at what Blue was holding in his hand.

'The rest of us started tucking ourselves away, although none of us had spewed our stuff. But not Blue. He didn't bat an eyelid. He stared her fair and square as she came closer.

'"That's a fair weapon you've got there, boy," she said. "I've seen a few, but not all that many as good as what you got there."

'Blue was cool. Didn't bat an eyelid. "Cut the crap, babe. I ask again, what you want to do with it?"

'That woman, who made her living giving men exactly what they wanted, seemed to quiver from head to toe.

'At first I thought she must be ill or something. Then I realised that this dame was panting for what my brother was showing her. That fat tongue of hers ran over her lips again.

'"Honey," she said. "I could eat what you've got there!"

'I almost came in my pants when she said that. I guess the others did too. The very thought of it. A full grown woman sucking on my brother's pistol! Wow, that's what I call a cocktail!

'Blue didn't give any sign that he was impressed by what she'd just said to him. He smiled that slow smile of his – the one that turns one side of his mouth up higher than the other.

'"Help yourself, baby." That's what he said. "Help yourself."

'The look on her face! She was all for it. She went down on her knees. I was as excited as anyone, and jealous as hell that Blue was going to get a piece of real hot action. I imagined how het up he was feeling. It took me by complete surprise when he suddenly grabbed hold of her hair. Her hands were already folded around his stem, but her mouth was a good six inches short of target.

'"You suck. They fuck," he said and nodded at the rest of us.

'My knees began to shake. My cock went so stiff, it shot back out the front of my pants. Luckily, my buttons were still undone or they'd have flown off and done some damage with that sort of force behind them. The others, I could see, felt much the same.

'Lucy blinked in our direction, but it was fast. Her eyes went right back to Blue's pistol.

'"OK," she muttered. We watched in amazement as Blue's cock disappeared into her mouth.

'Blue half closed his eyes and I could see he was enjoying what she was doing. Then, he opened them again and looked at the rest of us who were standing there with our gobs open.

'"What are you guys waiting for?"

'He jerked his head in the direction of her behind.

'I looked at one of the other guys, and he at me. We both looked at her skirt as though we had no idea what to do. Of course, we knew what to do really, but this all seemed so sudden. Like most young fellas, we'd all spun a few tall tales about how we'd had it with Daphne or Daisy or whoever at the back of the store, but hell, most of it was bullshit. Now it was for real.

'Me and the other guy grabbed for her skirt and hoisted it up over her back. Our cocks stood to immediate attention when we saw she wasn't wearing any underwear. But then, why should she? A woman in her trade had to be prepared and underwear would only get in the way of all that.

'One of the other guys, a guy called Speck, touched her first, then me and the other guy who'd hoisted her skirt did the same. We ran our hands over her ass, then slid it between her legs. She wasn't particularly wet and ready, but hell, we didn't know too much about them sort of things then. All we knew was that Blue had arranged for us to have pussy – our first.

'After each of us had given her a good feel, Speck lined himself up to give it to her. Two short shoves, and that was it.

'"My turn," I shouted as I shoved the other guy out of the way.

'I looked at Blue as I pushed it into her. Pleasure was written all over his face, but also something like endurance. It came to me then that what was happening to him was as good as what I was doing. But I also knew he was controlling himself; holding himself back until he was sure each of us had shot his load.

'Like him, I was pretty damned determined that it wouldn't be over too quickly. I was hell-bent on enjoying it.

'My old man used to have that saying that if God made anything better, he kept it to himself. At that moment, at that time, I felt as if I was God and I was savouring the fruits of my labour. Hell, it was good. You know what I mean?'

The others didn't comment. They knew Tony wasn't expecting one. Judging by his flushed cheeks and the tone of his voice, he was feeling what he had felt then all over again.

'Obviously, I couldn't hold it back. Can you blame me? After all, I was only a kid and this was the first time. On top of that, Paddy, the guy who I'd pushed past to get into her, had her blouse undone and was playing with her tits. Speck had joined him. After squeezing and pulling them about a bit, they tucked their heads under and sucked on her teats. I felt her muscles tighten round me when they did that. I felt her get juicy too and push her ass back against me. Boy, but did it feel good.

'That was it. The thought and sight of what everyone else was doing and what I was doing myself, was too much. Up and out it came and I groaned, and I cried, and I just felt as weak as a baby, my plug still in her hole, my come shooting into her.

'But I wasn't there for long. Patrick left his breast sucking and pushed me to one side. I slid out, and he slid in easily, and because Lucy was loving what we were doing to her, she helped him come in no time.

'Her whole body seemed to ripple like the wind pushing water. She made noises, and for a minute I thought she was choking. Then I saw Blue. His head was thrown back. His eyes were closed. He made a low sound – like a distant train signal. Not a muscle moved. Not until he relaxed and opened his eyes.'

Tony shook his head and began to laugh. 'That's when I knew my brother was a sex machine. A bit like a car.'

'How come?' asked Verecchia, a bead of sweat perched precariously above his brow.

Tony's laugh mellowed to an affectionate smile. 'Something that springs into life when the right key is turned, and gets to where it's going time and time again.'

'Sex or the car?' asked Ice.

'Both,' stated Prof, 'though my opinion, for what it is worth, is that a better description of Blue Bonecci would be sexual athlete rather than sex machine. Blue is always controlled, and I found that out on the first occasion I met him . . .'

Chapter 4

'The Eighteenth Amendment had really taken hold, and like a lot of people, I didn't take kindly to obeying a law that I thought infringed my civil liberties.

'I was a green grunt in the office of the DA then, and although I had a mind to get to the top and topple Dag Bernstein from his perch, I didn't quite have the connections to do it. But anyway, after a day of a warm office and sticky papers, I had a need for a drink and a place to unwind. I'd heard about some speakeasy down on seventh, and despite such places being officially out of bounds to me, I took the view that what the top brass didn't know, they wouldn't grieve over.

'The White Wand Club looked nothing more than a faded green door at the bottom of a flight of iron steps. I knew that at one time the steps had been made of wood, but I guess the clang of shoes on iron can be heard better. Security rests on such things.

'I knocked at the door and a small shutter opened no more than six by six. A pair of staring eyes looked out at me. The guy they belonged didn't say a word. In fact, he didn't even blink.

'Harold sent me.'

'Harold who?' the guy asked.

'The Peddlar.'

'My answer resulted in the shutter slamming down then I heard the bolt slide back. Being immersed in the administrative side of the DA's office had distinct advantages. I thanked my lucky stars that I'd taken the opportunity to study Harold Pederman's file before I'd come out. His nickname of "The Peddlar" was the key that got me in.

'I knew I was taking a chance both with my job and the guys that ran this place, and half wondered whether I should turn around and get on out of there. How about my career? Nuts, I thought to myself. I wasn't getting anywhere down town, and I certainly didn't want to be one of those lawyers who shuffles papers and deals with legal administration and municipal law all their lives. A drink, I decided, would help me unwind and decide what I should do next in my legal career.

'I sauntered into the joint just as a jazz trio had struck up a rip-roaring tune. I did my best to look unimpressed. But it wasn't easy, I can tell you. The White Wand might have had a shabby front door, but inside it hit you between the eyes. This was no cheap joint. The smell of perfume, rich Havanas and high calibre hooch made me feel excited. It was the kind of feeling you get when you're a kid and on your first visit to Santa Claus.

'I did a quick scan of the place. I remember wondering whether the walls were made of gold. It was only later, once I'd settled down at the bar and had a drink in my hand, that I realised they were gold in colour, but lacquered. It was the overhead lighting – a kind of sparkly affair of chipped glass – that made it shine like it did.

'I heard some broad ask me to buy her a drink. I'd been so busy taking in the details of the place I hadn't noticed her homing in on me. She had big blue eyes and a purple turban wound tight around her head. She sucked on a cigarette holder, pursing her lips as she looked up at me and fluttered those baby blue eyes.

'"Are you going to buy me a drink or what?" she asked.

'I remember stammering a bit at first. My experience with women was minimal. But I got her a drink anyway. I know now that she was a patsy. I bought her a drink, I had another. Each drink I drank, she got a cut. But I didn't know that then. I was just glad to have someone to talk to about my troubles. Besides, she smelt delicious. Her perfume was like a drug. The more I breathed it in, the more it filled my head. I drank more too. The more I drank, the more I let loose about how unhappy I was in my job at the DA's office and how I thought I had the makings of a really good DA, if someone would just give me the chance.

'I vaguely recall a certain look coming to her eyes just then, but didn't give it too much account. I was too wrapped up in myself and my opinion to notice anything much.

'"Never you mind, honey," she said and patted my arm. "We just might be able to do something about that. I think I know someone who might be able to pull a few strings for you."

'I don't remember quite what I said then. I only remember taking a swig from my glass as she sauntered off to a table that was half hidden behind some curtains.

'Her hand landed on my arm just as I was ordering another drink. It might have been my eighth drink, or it might just as well have been my tenth. Either way, she was back.

'"I want you to meet someone," she said. She got the glass out of my hand and put it down on the bar. Then she slid her hand into mine and led me over to the table by the curtain. That's when I first met Blue. I can't help remembering the directness of his look and the hint of a smile.

'"Hi there," he said, and shook my hand. "Take a seat, mister. I understand from little Chloe here that you're a man who wants to go places. Well, so do I, mister. I've got a feeling we can help each other out."

'I sat down, not quite knowing what I was letting myself in for, but being faintly aware that I was putting myself in a compromising situation. I thought about getting out of there. Then I caught the whiff of Chloe's perfume and face powder. She was standing real close to me. Then she wrapped her arms round me and sat on my lap. Any thought about leaving went clean out of my head. I was staying, no matter what.

'My mind went fuzzy with details just then because Chloe was nibbling at my ear. Blue was talking. The more Chloe nibbled at my ear, the more what Blue said seemed to make sense.

'Yes, I did deserve due credit for my work. I did deserve to rise through the ranks. "And I can help you," he said.

'My brain was jumping. Not only did I feel at ease with this guy, but Chloe had now slid her hand into my shirt and beneath my vest. Her fingers were icy cold and silky on my chest. I loved it.

'Blue leaned forward. "You can have anything you want – if you set your mind to it. You can do anything you want. It's all a matter of control."

'I didn't know quite what he meant, and besides, Chloe was sliding down between my knees beneath the table. My first thought was that she'd had too much to drink and was passing out. I know now that nothing could be further from the truth. Hostesses drink cold tea that's priced the same as Bourbon. They have to keep their heads. They have to earn their keep.

'At first, I tried to slap her hands away when she started fiddling with my fly buttons. I looked at Blue, then looked down at her. Blue smiled.

'"Let her get on with her job, and we'll get on with ours. Now. Once you've told me your name, we can get down to business. You can tell me exactly where you want to go, and I can tell you exactly what I want to know. Is that clear?"

'I could hardly believe he was saying this. There was this broad pulling my cock from my trousers and wrapping her mouth around it, and there was this guy smiling and looking at me as though we were sitting in the board room of some bank or big-shot company.

'Everything else seemed a fuzz. I can't even remember the faces of the two guys with him.'

'Probably Tiger Ted and Chinese Louie,' Verecchia interrupted. 'They were with him at the start. Used to be their outfit in fact, but Blue changed all that.'

Prof nodded.

'You're probably right. I don't really remember. All I do remember is telling him my name, and him saying he

23

preferred to give me a name he identified with someone who looked like me.'

'The Professor,' Tony interjected. 'Right? He said you looked like college professor.'

'Wrong. He said I looked like some professor in the movies. They're always pretty skinny, have little hair and wear glasses. That's how that came to be.

'Anyway. As I was saying. There was him talking business, and there was this woman taking me into her throat. I was sweating. My mouth must have looked like a drive-in cave. I was having trouble bringing my lips close enough to speak. But I certainly got the gist of what Blue was saying. You scratch my back, and I'll scratch yours. In other words, he had pull high up in City Hall, and he'd make sure I got up to where I belonged.

'I tried to thank him in words, but I came just as I was trying to get it together.

'"Don't worry," he said as I made the sort of noise you do when you've just had one hell of a good blow-job. "I can see how grateful you are." He grinned and looked at Chloe as she popped up from under the table. At the very same time, another girl with red hair and a freckled face appeared above the table on his side, her lips sticky with the same stuff that was round Chloe's mouth.

'You could have tipped me off that chair there and then. That guy had sat there as cool and calm as you like and spouted business whilst he was getting exactly the same treatment as I was. And there was me hardly able to get a word out because I was so aware of that girl sucking me off.

'I knew then that this guy was something else. This was

24

a man who was always in control, no matter what. Getting to be DA was going to be a cinch.

'The rest of the night passed in a haze. More drinks came and eventually I passed out and didn't come to until I woke up in my own bed. For a moment, I wondered whether I had dreamed everything. I took my cock out and sighed as I saw the smears of lipstick up and down its length.

'Laying back, I tried to recall my last impression of Blue Bonecci. The picture that came to mind was enough to make me hard again. I remember seeing both girls go down on hands and knees and crawl back beneath the table. Even though I was too drunk to be completely sure, I saw the sparkle in Blue's eyes. Apart from that, there was no sign whatsoever that two young women were playing with his prick as a whole speakeasy drank and danced to the throb of a black-faced jazz trio.'

Verecchia chuckled. 'A man of many talents. I like to think I had some influence on his career. It can honestly be said that I opened his eyes to many aspects of the sexual urge in men and women.'

'My brother's no faggot!'

Only the quick intervention of Ice stopped Tony from flying at the beaming Italian.

Verecchia raised one podgy hand. Gold rings glittered on each plump finger.

'You misunderstand, my dear boy. I am not saying that your brother's appetites were in any way similar to my own. But he had bought into a specialist concern that I owned and he wanted to see what he was getting for his money, so I took him there.'

Verecchia's smile was so wide, it seemed his eyes were in danger of disappearing in fat. His teeth were white and not dissimilar to a set of piano keys.

He nodded like an oriental sage. 'I think I can safely say your brother enjoyed the experience. But don't take my word. Judge for yourself . . .'

Chapter 5

'On certain nights of the week, Diocletian's caters for men only. What I mean by that is, both the performers and the audience are entirely male.

'In order for you to get the picture of what it looked like on the night I took Blue there, I will attempt to describe what it looks like on those other nights.'

Tony shifted in his chair as if trying to ease himself a little further away from the overweight Italian. The Prof sat a little more upright; a little more alert. Ice remained unmoved.

Eyes glittering, Verecchia licked his lips, aware that all three men must be feeling a little uncomfortable, though Ice alone gave little evidence of that.

'The Diocletian has pillars everywhere – just like the Romans did. Usually, I've got nubile young men facing those pillars, their hands chained above their heads, and cute little strips of cloth separating their buttocks. Any member of the audience is entitled to stroke them if they wish. None of the young men will complain of such handling.'

The fat Italian licked his lips, relishing the moment a while before continuing.

'Anyway, I took Blue there on a couples' night. That is, men and women, some of whom have been married to each other for years.

'Just like on the other nights, there are nubile bodies chained to the pillars, except that some are female. But they're dressed more or less the same and wear nothing apart from the strips of cloth that pass between their cheeks.

'I had always noticed that some of the women stroked the girls just as much as the men. I also noticed that some scratched or pinched the girls. Some even slapped them a few times and left patches of redness on their pretty white flesh. But no one complained. After all, everyone was there to immerse themselves in whatever decadence they wished to explore, but of course, I am not one to pass up a good business opportunity. I explained this to Blue. I told him I intended to put on a cabaret. A very special cabaret. He was intrigued.

'"What have you got in mind?' he asked me, I told him to be patient, but assured him he would be delighted at what he was about to see. It was like nothing he had ever seen before. When he looked at me, I could see the disbelief in his eyes.

'"There's not much I haven't seen," he said.

'"Wait," I said to him. "Wait and you will." I pointed to a wooden couch in the middle of the stage, It had leather belts and other things hanging from it. He didn't know, but I knew that it could be set up on end and used in a variety of other ways.

'The music started and four dancers leapt under the spotlights and whirled around the bed. They wore leather

28

corsets that were no more than a strip between their legs, a belt around their waists and straps that kind of scooped beneath their breasts and went over their shoulders. They also wore high boots that came half way up their thighs and were attached by suspenders to their belts. On their heads they wore Roman-style helmets with leather visors that came down over their eyes. Each of them carried a whip, and as they danced, they cracked them in time to the band.

'The effect was incredible. All conversation ceased. All eyes were on the dancers. The music stopped, and the whole room was so quiet, so still, a feather could have dropped and still been heard. One of the dancers made a pronouncement.

'"Someone here is unfaithful. Someone here has been untrue."

'She marched up and down as she said it. I could almost hear the audience breathing.

'"This is not right!" She cracked the whip. "She must be punished." She cracked the whip again. Another dancer came to her side.

'"Wait. It's not up to us to say she should be punished. It's up to them." She pointed at the audience. The other dancer then nodded.

'"You're right. It is up to them. Well? What do you say? Should this unfaithful woman be punished?"

'A mixed response came from the audience.

'The chief dancer spoke again. "I say this adulteress should be stripped naked and punished by other women. Do you agree with this?"

'Obviously, put like that, the whole audience was in

29

complete accord – especially the men. "*Yes!*" went up the cry. "*Yes! Yes! Yes!*"

'Two of the girls stepped forward and grabbed a woman from the audience. She struggled and called out that she was innocent. I remember her hair was red and she had it in some kind of bun that came adrift because she was struggling so much. She looked terrified, crying out that it wasn't her, that they had the wrong woman. They asked the man the woman had been sitting with if it was true that they had the wrong woman. Well, he wasn't going to spoil the fun, was he? His eyes were on stalks and he was almost dribbling.

'The girls went on with their job. They stripped the girl, tilted the couch up on end. Then they asked the audience how many strokes of the whip she should have. I think they decided one from each girl – just for starters.

'The first stroke landed. The girl screamed, so they gagged her. Her bottom was quite red after four strokes. Then they turned her over so that her belly, her breasts and her sex were on full view to the audience. You could almost hear them salivating, and you didn't need much imagination to know that there were more than a few stiff pricks and wet crotches in the audience.

'"This is what you want, isn't it?" one of the leather-clad girls said to the one tied up. She squeezed the girl's breast and played around with her nipple. Another girl did the same to the other breast. The other two began to play with her sex, dividing her lips so that the audience could see everything.

'Well, there was no way the girl could possibly ignore that sort of treatment. They were playing with all the right buttons, and within no time, the girl's hips were jerking against their fingertips. The audience burst into applause.

'Then the girls announced that if she'd been unfaithful with one lover, she might as well have more. They asked who wanted to be first to fuck her.

'Blue had stood silently beside me all this time. Now he stepped forward. Like everyone else, I clapped as he made his way down to the stage. He asked for the girl to go down on all fours. The girl's attendants got her into position, holding her in place as Blue unbuttoned himself and went into her. Of course, he didn't need to worry about making her come again. As he jerked himself into her, one of the attendants took care of the girl's pussy, whilst two more took care of her breasts. The third played with Blue's balls. It was mind blowing, but Blue controlled himself. He let it last as long as he wanted it to last.

'We had champagne after. I remember laughing and calling Blue a real stud, an Italian stallion.

'That man's sure got some energy. Do you know, we went on from there to a meeting with Big Circ, and Blue was on the ball as always. Big Circ tried to screw us on price for the Canadian shipments, but Blue was having none of it. Circ started high, Blue started low. By the end of it, the price was agreed and Circ got his ass back up over the border to Toronto.'

Verecchia smiled, his thick lips almost seeming to split his face in two.

'Helluva guy, that Blue. Only guy I know whose pecker works independently of his mind.'

Ice moved away from the mantelpiece where he had been

leaning and bent to take a Havana from a box on the desk.

Tony was saying something else about his brother as Ice rolled the cigar and walked over to the window. He lit the cigar, took a puff. He drew the curtain back a few inches and looked through the nets to the empty street below.

It had rained earlier and the pavement and road were wet. Pools of light thrown by streetlights and windows gleamed among the darkness.

A dot of redness glowed in the shadows then was gone. Something solid moved in the shadows, shifted very slightly and became a man.

Ice saw the cigarette glow as whoever stood in the doorway enjoyed what he could of his lonesome vigil.

'Anyone out there?'

The Prof was right behind him.

Ice let the curtain slip from his hand.

'No,' he replied. 'Just an empty street.'

He took hold of the DA's shoulder and eased him back into the room.

'Seeing as our Italian friend brought up the subject of Canada, let me tell you something about that little hunting trip Blue and I made a few months ago.'

Chapter 6

Ice went back to leaning on the mantelpiece and Prof, intrigued, returned to his seat.

Because of his height, Ice dominated the room, his shadow falling across the three others like that of some lean vulture just waiting to dive down and pick at their bones.

'As you know,' Ice began, his voice deep and as sonorous as the strict tempo of a slow beating clock, 'Blue and I went up into Alberta to join Redwood Jack and his boys, ostensibly to do a little business, but also to get in a spot of recreation.

'It was Autumn, and once the business was dealt with, we all shouldered shotguns and went up into the wilderness.

'I remember the air feeling like cold glass against my face, and already tasting a little frosty. But it was a good feeling. The trees were a mixture of yellow and orange against a bright blue sky, and I guess all us old boys were feeling pretty good.

'We were all wearing warm clothes and sturdy boots, and the twigs and bracken and stuff crackled beneath our feet. Redwood Jack and his boys were merry enough setting out, and so were we, but after a few miles of hard slog and a few bagged deer, me and Blue felt we'd had enough of the wild country.

'Redwood didn't mind, but him and his boys wanted to go further. Before leaving they showed us the trail to follow which would lead us back to the swank hotel we were staying at – you know, a real swell place set miles away from anywhere and half full of people wanting to escape the city, but not wanting to do without its comforts.

'As we walked back down, I happened to spot a nice little stag just waiting for me to bag. Blue told me not to bother, after all, it meant carrying a dead weight carcass all the way back down. But I decided to go for it anyway. Blue said he'd keep on walking.

'Anyway, to cut a long story short, I fired, the stag bolted, and at the same time, I heard Blue cry out. When I got to him, I found he'd slipped – hurt his ankle pretty bad.

'"Good job you missed that stag," he said. "You've got my carcass to get back down instead."

'I wrapped his ankle best I could. It was getting dark, and the trail was becoming indistinct, especially as it dipped into the shadows where the trees were.

'I don't know how it happened, and hate admitting to it, but we got well and truly lost. Night was falling fast, and I could hear sounds that I thought were grizzlies.

'Blue heard them too. As we stopped to take a breather, we discussed what to do – not that we had much option. We would keep going, and when we got to the first house we came to, we'd knock and ask if we could spend the night – money no object!

'We depended on guesswork to find the trail. There were

ferns growing to either side. Night was falling, and the trees meant things got dark pretty quick. Night sounds started up. Birds and insects mostly, but now and again we heard something larger. Perhaps a wolf. Perhaps a bear. I didn't confide my fears to Blue. I don't think I needed to. He could hear them as well as I could.

'We aimed our way towards a place where the trees thinned out. I was presuming there might be a clearing there. An ideal place where we could rest and light a fire. It was only as we got near to it that I caught a whiff of wood-smoke. I also smelt something cooking. The smell reminded me of new bread like my mom used to make.

'Blue and I stopped. We both sniffed, looked straight ahead, then at each other.

'"I can smell food," Blue said. I nodded and said yes. Our stomachs started making noises. Not surprising when you realise we hadn't eaten for about five or six hours. Knowing that help was close at hand kept us going. We came out of the trees and into a clearing.

'I heard her singing before I actually saw her. She was sitting in a rocker outside a log cabin. There were lights at the windows. I couldn't stop staring at them after all that darkness we'd come through.

'The cabin was a fair size. There were outhouses and piles of logs around them. Smoke curled from the chimney. Looked like something from a story book.

'She stopped singing and got up as she saw us stagger from the trees.

'"Can you help us?" I asked.

'She stood still for a moment. As she did so, the moon

came out from behind a cloud. The clearing was bathed in moonlight, and so was she. She had black hair down to her waist that looked blue in the moonlight. Slim. Long legs. She was wearing buckskin breeches and shirt. And moccasins. When I saw those, I realised she was Indian. I thought of that old saying about the only good Indian being a dead one, and thought what an idiot the guy who said that must have been.

'I called out to her that Blue was hurt. I asked her if she could help. She stood as though she was frozen. Then she moved towards us, her feet seeming to barely touch the grass.

'I explained about Blue's ankle, but wasn't very sure whether she was listening. Blue was staring into her eyes, and she was staring right back at him. She talked softly, asking where he hurt and whether we were both hungry. Her voice was . . .'

Ice paused. A faraway look came to his eyes as the memory of her voice echoed in his mind. It wasn't like Ice to be lost for words. His speech was always precise, his voice clear – like ice.

'Her voice was like the softness of fur against my skin. Only it wasn't against my skin. It was in my head. It made my whole body tingle.

'We went into the cabin where we got Blue onto the bed. I remember seeing the rough patchwork of the bedcover and thinking how simple it was, but how colourful.

'The Indian girl bathed and bandaged Blue's ankle. All the time she was doing it, I was seething with jealousy. I couldn't help it. At first sight, she had struck me that way.

'We ate warm bread, rabbit stew, and drank strong coffee.

The girl told us she had lived there with her father. He was dead now and she was all alone. She was glad we had come. She was lonely. After eating, Blue and me made it pretty obvious that we were tired.

'When the girl had gone outside, Blue had mentioned to me that there was only one bed in the room. We both eyed it, wondering what the chances were of one of us ending up with both the girl and the bed.

'When the girl came back in, we mentioned we needed to get to bed. Instead of offering to go outside while we undressed, she stayed and helped Blue get his trousers off. After that came his coat, then his other clothes until he was completely naked.

'He couldn't believe it. Neither of us could. But there he was, sitting there in his birthday suit as the girl pulled back the bedclothes.

'She turned round and looked at me. Her eyes were as big as pennies – big brown pennies. "Are you coming to bed?" she asked me. "You do not need my help with your clothes?"

'I showed no reaction. I merely said I could manage. She smiled then, and as I began to get undressed, she pulled off the buckskin shirt she was wearing. She wore nothing underneath. Her skin was like copper. Her nipples were a soft, dusky pink. I had a yearning to kiss them. I felt a thudding in my temple. Like any man, I was reacting to the beauty of her body. I could have had her then and there. Both of us could. And yet, neither of us made a move on her. We merely watched as she kicked off her moccasins and sent them scurrying across the earth floor. She unhitched her breeches then and slid them down over her thighs, her knees, and then off of her feet.

'Even before I got out of my trousers, my cock was stiff and proud. My eyes fastened on her belly and from there, went lower. That hair too had a tinge of blue about it. It looked silky, and I vaguely wondered how soft it would feel in my mouth, and how she would taste on my tongue.

'She turned her bottom towards me as she lifted her leg to climb into the bed. I saw Blue shift over. He hardly seemed to notice me. His eyes were fixed on her. Like me, his cock was a lot stiffer than his ankle.

'The girl threw me a smile over her shoulder, then slid into bed. By the time I slid in behind her, Blue had his arms around her. She was pressed tight against him, her back and her beautiful rock hard bottom towards me.

'The bed wasn't that wide, so my body touched hers. She felt so warm. So fuckable. Blue was already half way there. I felt his hands travelling down her back and over her behind. In an effort to be polite, I lay very still, hands behind my head.

'The girl rolled over onto her back, and Blue rolled over with her. A sudden jerking of the bed told me he was in her. I felt jealous. I felt sad. Somehow, I knew he wasn't right for her and she wasn't right for him. She was so natural. So wild. Like the night outside the windows. Like the forest and the animals howling at the moon.

'I might have pretended to be asleep, but then something completely unexpected happened. Blue was riding her, kissing her mouth and playing with her tits. Doing all the things I would like to do to her. Her hand brushed against me. My cock jerked. I gritted my teeth. Then I gasped as her fingers curled around it. I couldn't believe it. There she was with Blue making love to her, and at the same time, she was playing with me.

'As that dame pulled on my prick, I went in turn from warm to hot, to boiling point. She did incredible things with her thumb, her fingers, and the palm of her hand. I felt that I was in heaven. I closed my eyes, I opened them, I gasped and I sighed.

'I saw Blue looking at me. He looked as excited as I felt. He smiled as he rammed it into her. An unspoken agreement ran between us. He lowered his head onto her right bosom. I reached over and began to play with her left nipple.

'I saw Blue suck on her nipple, pulling it between his teeth so it stretched and went from pink to purple. I eased myself across the pillow. Her nipple was not far from my face, peeping out from between my finger and thumb. I could have sucked it then and there. But I didn't. She was looking at me, her eyes so big and so beautiful.

'I smelt her breath. It was sweet, like the smell of wild flowers. Her eyes dropped to my lips. My eyes dropped to hers. I kissed her. Not passionately. Not at first. But gently, slowly. They were like velvet, and so innocent. So young.

'My tongue went between her lips. The tip of my tongue met hers. They danced like snakes. I sucked on it. She sucked on mine.

'Her flesh was soft, like silk to touch. She kept her eyes tightly closed as I kissed her, but I wanted her to open them. I willed her to. But she didn't. Not until I transferred my mouth to her nipple did she open her eyes, and then all she did was look at Blue. You know, the way most women do. It was usual, but it hurt like hell.

'I spurted my load at about the same time as Blue. He filled her body and I filled her hand. We did it again that night. Blue kept coming. He also kept asking her to do it again. And she did. She was hypnotised by the guy. I shouldn't have minded that. After all, I was getting my share too. But I did mind. I did.'

Ice's cool, even voice fell to silence. His eyes were staring straight ahead of him, and yet it seemed he saw nothing of the room or the men gathered in it.

A vein throbbed in his temple. His jaw was firm set.

Verecchia shifted his big bulk in his chair.

'So? What happened next?'

Only the steel grey eyes of the tall man moved. They settled on the broad Italian, and there was no way any of them gathered could read the message in them. Ice was good at hiding his feelings – usually.

'We got up and got dressed the next day. We had breakfast too. Blue asked the girl to come with us. She said she'd think about it. Blue asked her again. Told her he wanted to see her again. The girl answered that she wanted to see him again too. But she needed time.

'She looked down at herself and began fiddling with that long black hair. I trembled when she did that. The night before I had felt it trailing over my belly as she'd leaned over me, her thighs spread over my pelvis.

'"I can't come with you," she said. "First, I have to look like a city girl. That will take time. I can't come with you looking like this."

40

'Blue cuddled her close. "Don't leave it too long," he said. "I want you with me, babe. I really do."

'I felt awkward standing there like that with Blue giving her his usual spiel. And yet, I knew that Blue was sincere. But only as sincere as he can be. Blue has his own yardstick for judging feelings.'

Ice stopped talking. The room seemed extra silent now each of them had spoken of Blue and their own personal experiences of his sexual athleticism.

Prof got out his pocket watch and glanced at the time. His chair squeaked as he moved.

Verecchia shook his head and cut the end off another cigar.

Tony, Blue's brother, grinned and began trimming his nails.

'That's my brother for you,' he said, a hint of pride permeating his voice.

Ice glanced briefly at the window, and then at Tony Bonecci.

'Yes, Tony boy. That's your brother for you.'

Chapter 7

'Una? Are you ready yet?'

She guessed it was Kitty knocking at the thin ply door which shivered under the onslaught of female fists.

At first she didn't answer. She wanted the moment to remain undisturbed. She was lying naked on the bed, one arm beneath her head, her flesh creamily warm in the glow of the single bulb behind the pigskin shade of the table lamp.

Her gaze was fixed on the ceiling. But she wasn't seeing the dead paintwork and the naked lightbulb whose shade had only disintegrated the day before. She was seeing only what had been and what might have been.

'Una! We're going to be late.'

The door handle rattled as Kitty shook it from the other side. Una's eyes slid sidelong and watched the key jiggle in the lock. Kitty was always so damned punctual, and sometimes she was glad of it, and sometimes she was not. At this moment in time, she wanted to be alone with her own thoughts for a while longer.

'I won't be long. Half an hour. That's all.'

For a moment the sound of her own voice took her by surprise. It had a muffled quality about it as if her surroundings were strangling or suffocating it.

'Are you alright?' she heard Kitty ask.

She cleared her throat before replying. 'Sure. Give me half an hour.'

She heard Kitty give an exasperated sigh and heard a mumbled, 'Suit yourself!'

Even before the tapping of Kitty's footsteps on the threadbare linoleum had disappeared, Una's thoughts had turned back to Blue.

In an effort to imagine him more clearly, she closed her eyes, took a pillow from beneath her head and cuddled it against her body. She sighed happily. The coarse cotton was cool against her skin.

Nipples that had tingled in response to the thoughts in her mind, now hardened. Her stomach muscles tightened and her skin began to tingle in expectation as her hips rose slightly from the bed.

Her breath came in short, sharp gasps and she moaned just as she had with him. She longed for his touch; for his hands to delve beneath her buttocks and raise her closer to him. She ached for his lips to suck at her nipples, the tip of his tongue to lick her flesh.

Squeezing her eyes tightly, she tried to forget that she had ended up in a seedy room in a run down brownstone in an area where washing hung high from apartment windows, and women sold their bodies for food rather than pleasure.

Reality punctured her imagination when she came to that moment when his body would have entered hers. In long, curling strokes, she ran her fingers over her belly and beneath the pillow. Her hips rose from the bed and she purred with pleasure as her nails tangled in the moist welcome of her pubic hair.

It was only her finger that eased the ache between her legs. Easing it into the warm flesh, she pretended she was him, imagined how the slick wetness of her open body felt upon *his* finger, *his* lips, *his* cock.

Opening her legs in welcome, she pushed at the small nub that hid like a rosebud between her damp lips. Pretending to be him was not easy but the response from her clitoris sent an over-powering message to her brain. The intoxicating sensations spread, intensifying, taking her over, making her writhe and jerk like a marionette on strings.

She cried out as she would have done with him, her hips jerking as spasm after spasm shocked her nerve endings and shook her flesh.

For a moment she lay still, her eyes closed. The pillow that lay on top of her was warmer now, just as his body would have been.

Her breasts rose and fell rapidly against it before her breathing returned to normal. Soon, she would have to open her eyes and the foolishness, the shame of what she had just done, would be laid bare.

The moment of truth was put off as long as possible, but not indefinitely. Kitty would be back soon and the illusion would be completely shattered, just like her dreams.

A sob started way down inside her. She tried to swallow it, tried to tell herself she didn't care that Blue didn't love her any more. But the sob would not be swallowed like a mouthful of bread or a forkful of steak. It rose up inside her, lay heavy at the back of her throat.

Tears squeezed out of her closed eyes.

She rolled over and cuddled the pillow to her as the sob became a sound.

Face buried in the pillow, she muffled what she could of her despair, cuddled the pillow to her, and drew up her legs as the sobs became cries.

Hell hath no fury . . . The words came unbidden into her mind. What was the rest of the saying?

. . . like a woman scorned.

At that moment, the ache in her body seemed to ignite. Behind despair came anger, and behind that came hate.

She wiped her face against her pillow, opened her eyes and took in the shabby details of the room; the painted washstand; the pigskin shade on the tarnished lamp; the sink and cooker separated only by a thin yellow curtain from the area she slept and lived in.

One man had brought her to this. One man. Blue Bonecci.

No fury . . . Una thought to herself as the sound of Kitty's heels came from the other side of the door.

Swinging her legs off the bed, she slung the pillow back into its place and dabbed at the wetness around her eyes.

'Be right there, Kitty.'

She turned the key and rushed to the sink to sponge away the tears from her eyes and the stickiness of self abasement from between her legs.

Kitty swept in, accompanied by the soft hush of the pink satin dress she was wearing that suited her bobbed brown hair and cocker spaniel eyes, but looked at odds with the shabbiness of the room.

Although she was only twenty-two, Kitty had the ways

of someone twice that age. Although large, her eyes had the look of someone who'd seen most of what the world had to offer. The hard dimples at the ends of her mouth gave the impression she hadn't seen much of life worth having. But the way she moved, the sway of her bony hips, and the petulant thrusting of her boyish posterior was like she was cocking a snoot at the world, saying 'Hey! I don't think much of you, but hell, I sure am going to make the most of it.'

With guilty swiftness, her eyes ran over Una's body before fixing on the sweetheart face and the clear blue eyes.

'You been crying?' she asked, her voice an odd mix of southern drawl and streetwise Chicago.

Una turned swiftly away. 'Don't be silly!'

As though time had suddenly stuffed two hours into one, she pushed past her worldly-wise friend, grabbed a pair of black stockings and matching garters from the chair and sat on the bed.

Gaze fixed on her red-painted toes, Una began rolling a silky, crisp stocking over her foot.

With the raised eyebrows and knowing nod of someone not easily fooled, Kitty folded her arms and leaned against the wall.

'Forget him, Una, He's a bastard. Where other men have a roving eye, Blue Bonecci has a roving prick. Everyone knows it.'

Una paused and took a deep breath. Each word was a wound, the statement a series of stabs that left her body feeling sore, though the real pain remained deep inside.

Feeling foolish, used and unwanted caused an angry

pinkness to flush her cheeks. Before her own eyes, she saw her knuckles go white.

'He said he loved me.' Her shoulders slumped. The words seemed so unsatisfactory. So empty.

Kitty shrugged. 'He probably did when he was fucking you. But what's love got to do with sex? Why, Blue's the sort that can roll on and roll off and say the same thing to every babe he sticks.'

'Everything!' Una's eyes blazed. 'Love has everything to do with it, otherwise, why say it?'

Kitty shook her head. 'Not to Blue it doesn't. Blue can feel affection for one woman, yet still want to take another to bed. To him it's like eating and drinking. Something you just have to do.'

Una hurried her garter up over her leg and immediately began pulling on the other stocking. There was a quiet moment between them, the sort that comes along when two people are looking at the same subject in different ways.

'I thought about going home,' Una muttered.

Kitty looked surprised. 'You wouldn't, would you?'

Una glanced up. 'I only thought about it. Then I thought, why should I? There's no one there. I'd be alone.'

Kitty glanced at the pretty breasts that were round, firm and tipped with upturned nipples of palest pink. Like damask roses, she thought before swiftly looking away.

She looked again as Una stood up, her body looking more vulnerable, more naked somehow because she was only wearing black stockings and garters of black velvet.

A posy of pubic hair as soft as velvet and as shiny as silk lured Kitty's gaze down to parts of Una's body she should not be looking at. It was hard to tear her gaze away and force down the feelings that simmered gently deep inside. The feelings frightened her, made her excited, made her nervous. Men she had had in plenty, yet never had they aroused her like Una did. But Kitty had never voiced how she felt. Una was her friend and she wanted her to remain so.

'So what are you going to do?' Kitty spoke slowly, as if she didn't really want to know the answer.

'Look!' Una cried, stretching out her arms. 'Look what I've come to.'

'You didn't have to come here. You could have stayed with him.'

Una rounded on her. 'And done what? Watch from the shadows each time he took some other woman to bed?'

She clenched her fists and let out one strangled sob. Her silky black bob tickled the nape of her neck as she threw back her head.

'I couldn't stand it, Kitty. I just couldn't stand it.'

'Oh, baby!' In one stride, Kitty was at her side. 'There, there.' Kitty wrapped her arms around her and held her close, stroking Una's silky back as the dark haired girl rested her head on her shoulder.

'Blue Bonecci is not an easy man to understand,' Kitty began. 'But he's not unlike a lot of guys in this city. In fact, a lot of the mob bosses are just like him, yet they still have families; still have girlfriends too.'

Una said nothing. The feel of the pink satin dress against her body, and the soft hands caressing her back and smoothing her hair gave her comfort.

'Let me tell you a story, to take your mind off him,' Kitty began softly. 'It's about one of the toughest guys Chicago's ever known . . .'

Chapter 8

'Roberto Farneccio had come over with his father from Sicily when he was not much more than a baby in arms.

'Like most immigrants, he entered through Ellis Island, a place which swarmed with more insect life than a hive of bees, which in turn necessitated sudden spurts of DDT and questions about personal health rather than social background.

'Italian, Swedish, Irish brogue and Yiddish echoed over crowded alleys that bore no resemblance to the streets of gold the immigrants had hoped for.

'"New York is like a post office," Senor Farneccio had told his son. "It is a place only for letters to arrive and be sorted. They are all still crowded together and have not yet found the individual letterbox they are destined for."

'With this in mind, Roberto's father moved his family to Chicago where they'd heard work was plentiful in the cattle yards by virtue of the fact that naturalised Americans had moved to well-paid jobs in the burgeoning motor car companies.

'His father decided that would suit him for a while until he got something else under way. "Ok, so the work smells.

But so does the food we eat. That smells pretty good to me, and anyway, it won't be forever. In time, I will get something else under way."

'Through the working week, he smelt of his job; the lingering stench of sweating steers. At weekends, when the wind was blowing in the right direction, the fetid smell squeezed beneath closed doors and seeped through cracks in the walls and holes in the roof.

'Unfortunately, Senor Farneccio never did get anything else under way, and his family lived in pretty poor conditions until Roberto decided to strike out on his own. By the time he was twenty, he was one of the most successful gang leaders in the city, already earmarked by the FBI, and feared by others who followed the same violent and dishonest road as he did.

'He had it all. He had the money, the house, the cars and the women.

'Then he met Sophia. She was introduced to him by his mother. Sophia's family had just come over from the old country and they figured that by setting up a connection with a successful immigrant family, they would prosper. Successful, in their eyes, meant there was a square meal on the table every day of the week.

'Sophia was only sixteen years old and had big brown eyes, long brown hair, and was as sleek and leggy as a two-year-old colt.

'Roberto had barely even held her hand before they were married. The families were pretty strict on that, preferring to accept the civil liberties of the New World, but not its morals. Sophia would be chaperoned until the day she married, and regardless of her husband's sexual experience, she would arrive a virgin at the altar.

'And so it was that Roberto Farneccio married the pretty little girl from Italy who had never lain with a man, nor even allowed one to kiss her.

'Roberto himself had gained experience from the backstreets around the cattle pens where ten cents could buy ten minutes of bliss.

'Roberto usually paid more than the basic rate, but expected more than the standard service in return. And that's all he did get. He gave them money, not affection, and in return he received sexual relief.

'But the little girl fresh from Naples knew nothing of her fiancé's sexual predilections. She saw only a honey-gold complexion, sleek black hair, and eyes like brown velvet. He was her bridegroom and she was his bride.

'Sophia was a picture in white and happy as can be. She knew little about her new bridegroom except that he loved her, she loved him, and her family approved of the marriage. Everyone was happy.

'But of course, Sophia was also a virgin. It was accepted by the family and by Roberto himself that it was of paramount importance that a wife should be a virgin. A husband was expected not to be. After all, he was the one to do the doing wasn't he?

'On their wedding night, once the kisses became more demanding, and Roberto had started to remove her nightdress, Sophia was getting nervous.

'With all the refinement of an indulged child with a new toy, Roberto played with her breasts, then tore her nightdress from her body as if it were made of nothing more substantial than tissue paper.

'He pushed her back on the bed, then lay on top of her, forcing his knee between hers as he kissed hungrily at her mouth before thrusting his cock into her. Sophia was devastated. Foreplay was a thing Roberto associated with golf, and her crying out in pain as he burst through her hymen cut no ice with him, except to confirm that he was the first man to enter.

'Sore and tearful, Sophia lay still once he was satiated and snoring, wondering how often she would be expected to lie under him and put up with his fierce intrusion and rapid ejaculation.

'If this was being a wife, she didn't think very much of it.

'But duty overruled self, and soon a little *bambino* was on the way. After that, came a second *bambino* and a third.

'Sophia began to put on a little weight like a lot of Italian women do, and although she realised her man wasn't quite the Romeo she had expected, she was as loyal to him as any wife should be. When she found out she was pregnant with her fourth child, she decided to surprise him with the news.

'Because of the nature of his business, it wasn't very often he was home at nights. Sophia had accepted that. Her husband was a very important businessman, he provided very well for her, and he looked after the people closest to him.

'He fixed things for people, people like her own brother who wanted to be in charge of the local branch of the stock drovers' union.

'Roberto had fixed it. The guy who had been in charge

was getting too old for the job any way. He had refused to retire after Roberto had told him he should, but it came as no surprise to anybody that he had fallen down the stairs shortly after that and broken his legs, so the job became vacant. Roberto immediately suggested his brother-in-law for the position, and no one had opposed him.

'Then there was Clementina, Roberto's niece, who wanted to be in a Broadway show.

'The impresario in charge of the production had turned her down for a singing and dancing role. Apparently, he'd mistaken her for someone else, because shortly after that, he'd asked her to take the lead role because the girl picked for the job had gone and got herself pregnant. No one knew who the father was, but the girl was rushed out of town, and it was rumoured that her mind had been affected by the shock of it all.

'But because she was expecting her fourth child, Sophia took it in her head to go and announce it to her husband as a birthday surprise. He would be thirty-eight years old shortly, and she knew he would be pleased about having another child. But first, she had to find him.

'Roberto kept a big diary in his drawer with an address list at the back. To locate him was simply a question of looking in his diary, taking a note of the initials, then looking at the address in the back.

'By this method, she found out where he was, and clasping a bottle of champagne in her hand, she took a taxi there.

'Unfortunately, the address was that of a whorehouse from which Roberto obtained a useful monthly return. Perhaps if he'd been inside the place when she arrived, the concierge on the door would have told her to go away and warned Roberto that his wife was trying to gain entry.

'As it was, Roberto was not inside, but sitting in his car outside.

'In an attempt to surprise him by shouting happy birthday and then by announcing that she was pregnant again, Sophia crept up on him. She grabbed the door handle, pulled it wide open and shouted her heartfelt wishes and joyful tidings through the opening. Roberto went white with shock, then red with anger.

'At first, Sophia couldn't understand his reaction. She kept her smile fixed. That is, until she saw another face look up at her from between her husband's legs.

'A naked girl was kneeling on the floor at the back of the limousine giving her husband head; her husband, with whom she had only laid on her back whilst he shoved his juice into her.

'She screamed, dropped the champagne and froze. Roberto got two of his henchmen to take her home.

'You can imagine the atmosphere in that house for the next few months.

'Roberto warned her never to follow him again. She was his wife and should know her place.

'She tried to get a promise from him that he would never have anything to do with loose women again.

'Roberto just laughed at her. Who did she think she had married, the Pope? What sort of business did she think he was involved in?

'Never before had Sophia really asked herself where the money came from. Now she realised that the clothes on her children's backs and on her own, the beautiful house they lived in, the cars and the jewellery, had not been gained by anything like honest sweat.

'Even so, she could have lived with that. It was the thought of being a loyal wife to a man who was a lousy lover that got to her the most. It came to her mind that what was sauce for the goose was also for the gander.

'Although she had put on some weight and was pregnant, Sophia was still determined to get some of the sensual pleasure she craved. But where was she to get this pleasure? The young man who worked in the delicatessen down the street came to mind. He was a tall, straight boy with dark curly hair and eyes that smiled the moment she walked into the shop. It didn't seem to matter to him that she was plump, married and had three children.

'She wondered if he fantasised about her in his bachelor bed, and it thrilled her to think he did.

'At a time when she knew her husband would be out of town, she arranged for the delicatessen to deliver her order. No one else was home. The maid was off for the day, and her children were with her mother-in-law.

'Her mother-in-law was quite happy with the idea and told her to lie down and rest whilst she could. Once the new baby arrived, she would have little time to herself.

'Before the young man arrived from the delicatessen, Sophia put on her sexiest outfit; a creamy satin *peignoir* with thin straps and a trimming of coffee-coloured lace. She dabbed perfume on her nipples before pulling the straps over her shoulders.

'The young man arrived, his eyes wide as he took in the

sight of her voluptuous body in an item of clothing that left nothing to the imagination. Although she tried to entice him into the bedroom, the young man refused to move.

'"Don't you want what you see?" she asked him as she slid her straps down over her curvaceous shoulders.

'He couldn't speak. He nodded, his eyes not leaving the mountainous breasts that were slowly coming into view.

'"Oh, yes!" he exclaimed, his eyes wide and his voice half strangled.

'She touched his cheek, her thumb stroking the corner of his mouth.

'He gasped, his mouth opening like a ripe fruit. She fastened her own mouth over his, sucking on his lips and his tongue as she pressed her breasts against his chest.

'Shaking with apprehension, his hands rose. He spread his fingers until of sufficient size to cover her breast. She trembled as her nipple dipped into his palm, her breath escaping in short, sharp gasps as he pressed, pinched and nipped at her nipples.

'Taking one breast in each hand, he kneaded them, pulled on them and pummelled the heels of his palms against them like a baker rolling dough.

'Their mouths stayed clamped together, and her belly slammed against his loins as he played with her nipples. She gave a little cry of surprise as he pulled his mouth away from hers.

'"They're wet," he said breathlessly between her profusion of kisses. "Your teats are wet."

'She guessed what it was. Although the baby was not expected for another four months, she was already lactating in readiness. But there was no mouth yet to suckle.

'And yet I have so much to give, she thought. She saw his finely arched brows crease in a deep frown as he studied the wetness that ran over his fingers.

'"Are you thirsty?" she asked him.

It was as though she had awakened him from a dream. He looked at her with a youthful, puzzled expression on his face.

'She smiled. "Suck me," she said softly. Placing her hand firmly on the back of his head, she eased it downwards.

'Clasping his head to her, she threw back her head and closed her eyes. He nuzzled between her nipples, then as though a forgotten memory had resurfaced in his mind, he began sucking.

'Slowly, she began rocking backwards and forwards, crooning to him as she would to a child. And all the while, he sucked, and made her feel good.

'As he swopped from one nipple to the other, she gave little moans which became more vocal as his teeth nipped, his fingers squeezed her ample breasts, and more milk spurted into his mouth.

'They never did get to the bedroom that first time, but she did go down on all fours on the kitchen floor. He got behind her, pulled her *peignoir* over her back and gasped with delight as he exposed her splendid ass.

'"What a beautiful big white ass," he murmured.

'He fondled it at first, tracing the crack in between and letting his fingers slide between her legs and dip into her juicy cleft.

'And all the time he did this, she murmured with pleasure,

forgot she was married, and thanked God she had found a man who could put into practice all the fantasies that came to haunt her at night when she lay beside her husband, unloved and unsatisfied.

'One finger explored at first, dipping into her wetness, turning around in her softness, plunging in, then drawing out so that her body made a soft, sucking sound. The first finger was joined by another and another until her portal was full of fingers.

'Sophia groaned. This, she decided, was how sex should be, two people indulging, exploring each other with eyes, fingers, lips, and tongue. There should be no boundaries, and no end to love-making until each participant was well and truly spent.

'Once his fingers had aroused her inner flesh to drip with fluid, he gripped her big thighs and shoved his prick into the juicy entrance that awaited him. Crisp, curly hair gently grazed her buttocks. Strong, sensitive fingers massaged her ample behind and wide thighs.

'She cried out as he lunged, withdrew, then lunged again, the kitchen table a blur before her eyes, the kitchen floor a smooth surface that might just as easily been a bed for all she cared.

'"I've got you at last," she heard him say against her ear. "I've been dreaming of this. Wanting to shoot it in you, over you. I've wanted to rub it into your belly, over your tits, see it dripping on your tongue. And now, I've got you, and now I can love you."

'Her eyes snapped open in surprise at what he said and at what she was feeling. For the first time ever, she knew what it was like to truly make love, not just to have sex. This was more than Roberto had given her. Much more.

'The young man with the curly hair cried out as he came into her, every vein on his neck standing proud as if about to burst out through his skin, tendons taut with power as blood surged along with orgasm through his veins.

'Sophia willed her own climax to linger, to allow her to savour every last indistinct tremor, every curling, swirling, ecstatic release of nervous energy and pent-up passion.

'Roberto had neglected her needs as a passionate woman. She was like a flower whose bud has never opened, a bird whose wings have never grown large enough to fly.

'Her husband had given her children, but denied her the pleasures he himself indulged in so freely. In short, Sophia wanted more of what she had missed.

'"Again," she demanded. "I want you to do it again."

'Leaning back against the table, with thumb and forefinger, she pulled her pubic lips apart so he could more easily feast his eyes on the plump pink flesh that was usually hidden from sight.

The curly haired young man examined the flesh between her legs with far more diligence and much more pleasure than any doctor had ever done, much less her husband.

'There was also a look in his eyes that Sophia dared to hope was adoration.

'Once she had aroused him by using her fingers and her mouth, she lay on the kitchen table, legs spread wide. As his penis entered her, he kissed her lips, gently at first, then with more demand, more vigour.

'Now and again, his mouth returned to her breasts, his

lips brushing her flesh, circling the large areolae as if awaiting her permission.

'"Suck me," she extolled, her voice strong, though racked with the breathlessness of someone who has entered a race and will die if she does not win.

'Sophia felt more satisfied with his mouth than at any time of feeding her own children.

'When she came this time, she closed her eyes and let the whole magnificent feeling flood over her, warming her toes, her ears, and all the places in between.

'Of course, she kept her liaison secret from Roberto. She also never used the bed when she was with Sam, the young man from the delicatessen.

'In fact, once the baby had been born, Sam and she used all sorts of different places in which to have sex.

'They did it in shop doorways. They did it in her car, in the storeroom out back of the delicatessen, in the elevator, even beneath a lone tree behind the freight yards.

'Roberto hardly seemed to notice any difference in his wife. After all, she had always lain still beneath him as he fucked her. So what was different?

'It just seemed to him that she was beyond his reach. As he thudded quickly into her, there was a vacant look in her eyes as if she were somewhere else entirely.

'He tried speaking to her as he fucked her. He even had half a mind to ask her if she'd like to try a different position, but quickly reminded himself that she was his wife and wives didn't do things like that.

'Nothing would have happened, if she hadn't started to lose weight. She hadn't actually tried to lose weight, it was just that by doing it so often with Sam she was expending much more energy than before. Soon, a new Sophia began to appear, or rather, she began to again be the leggy young woman she had once been. Of course, she wasn't quite as slender as at sixteen, but with maturity had come a sleek roundness to her breasts, her hips and even her limbs.

'Sophia had grown into a beauty.

'Roberto became jealous. He didn't want his wife to look like that. It suited him to come home, do his marital duty, and re-enter the twilight world he inhabited where any broad would suck his cock or bend over whilst he shoved it between the cheeks of her behind.

'In the Italian community, security was confirmed by the size of one's wife. She was the anchor of the family. The heavier she was, the greater the anchor.

'Roberto began to feel insecure. No man in his entourage of hoods would even dare to look at Sophia for fear of arousing his anger.

He issued a warning, though most of his associates had got the gist already.

'"Anyone who looks at my wife will have his cock cut off and shoved down his throat till he chokes."

'None dared look, and in the meantime, Sophia went on screwing her Sam.

'Eventually, she got pregnant again.

'Roberto was beside himself with joy. His wife would get fat with a baby in her belly, and he would feel gratified. Because a sense of security had returned with the announcement, Roberto showered her with flowers. Again, he thought to himself, she will balloon with motherhood, and even after the baby is born, she will be the family anchor again.

'Unfortunately for Roberto, things didn't quite turn out that way.

'Trouble was brewing between him and a rival gang for control of the red-light district of Chicago, and a cut from the protection rackets.

'A lot of blood was spilt, so much so, that both gang leaders at last decided to have a talk to settle their differences.

'Roberto went off to that meeting in all good faith. Uglio, his enemy, was there as he expected him to be along with his mob.

'No one made a move to upset the proceedings, although everyone was tooled up to the eyebrows. But the meeting was an ambush. Not one perpetrated by either side of the gathering, but by the team of G-men lying in wait for them.

'Not only was Roberto killed, but so was every member of the gang.

'Sophia was dry-eyed when they told her. They put it down to shock what with her having a baby and suchlike.

'Because Roberto was the don of the family, his mother took it upon herself to take his children under her roof. Sophia started to protest, but stopped herself.

'Unbeknown to everyone else, Roberto's death had come as something of a relief. Anxiety had been her constant companion ever since she had discovered she was pregnant again.

'She tempered her urge to protest about her mother-in-law taking the children. An instinct deep inside told her that the child she was carrying was not sired by Roberto. She didn't know quite how she knew. She just did.

'Despite the fact that most of Roberto's mob was wiped out, she knew she would attract revenge once the truth came out. She could not chance that.

'Under cover of darkness, she and Sam left Chicago and set out for the Canadian side of the Great Lakes. Sam's son was born there, which was just as well.'

Una raised her head from off the bed where they now lay.

'But how would her relatives had found out that the baby wasn't her husband's?'

Kitty smiled and kissed her forehead then her lips, and all the time her hands stroked the dark hair and the silky skin.

'It was like this. To Roberto, Sophia and the rest of the mob, the old country was either Italy or Sicily. Sam's origins were somewhere in darkest Africa.'

Immediately understanding her meaning, Una's lips formed a silent 'O'.

Kitty smiled, saw the pretty shape of Una's mouth and took advantage of it.

Although they should have presented themselves at the diner along the road for a job interview, neither of them bothered. Both had been aroused by Kitty's story, and whether it was true or not, Una needed someone to love her, someone to take Blue's place and make her feel better.

Chapter 9

Most people regarded Gloria as silly, but being silly certainly had its advantages.

Appearing silly was far better than appearing threatening, in her opinion. Silliness was ignored and laughed at, and along with weakness, brought out the more macho side of a man's nature. Not for her the alluring wickedness of the *femme fatale* who preferred to dominate men rather than have them dominate her. Power wore soft satin gloves as far as Gloria was concerned.

She first saw Blue Bonecci at the Scarlet Soul speakeasy, and immediately decided she wanted him. It didn't matter that he was with the dark-haired, sloe-eyed Una who moved like a snake and had less meat on her than a rib-eye steak.

Una, she'd found out, was the most long-lasting of all Blue Bonecci's women. Familiarity might not breed contempt in the man in her sights, but it might have bred the first traces of boredom.

Una was dark. Gloria was blonde. Una was slinky, dangerously alluring, whereas Gloria was bubbly and well-rounded. In short, she and Una were complete opposites.

Blue was sitting at a table with other guys when Gloria

first saw him. Una was sitting on the table edge, her chin high as she gazed at Blue beneath heavy-lashed eyelids. She held a cigarette holder in one hand, and as she smoked, she smiled an unchanging, secretive smile.

If she spoke or laughed, Gloria didn't hear her. Not that she really cared either way what sort of hold Una had over Blue. He was the man she wanted. What Gloria wanted, Gloria got. She could pout her way into a man's heart, wring the last vestige of sympathy out of him, and equally, the last dollar.

Diametrically opposed to Una, she was loud, Una more silent. Her skin white as milk, and her lips red as blood. She had ripe, full breasts, the hint of a belly, and the sort of buttocks that are singularly recognisable through the most clinging of dresses.

That first night when she'd set her cap at Blue, she wore a sparkling dress that was nothing much more than a mass of gold and red sequins. The tiny discs were sewn onto the merest cobweb of lace and would have scratched at her skin if it hadn't been pre-washed before being made.

Slyly, she had watched, soaking up the looks and comments of admirers until Una made her way to the powder room.

Her chance had come. She made her excuses to those men whose hands had strayed down her back or along her thigh as she'd waited for the right time.

Breasts bouncing, she hollowed her back so their presence became more noticeable. Red lips smiling, eyes sparkling, and half smoked cigarette replaced with a fresh one, she got to Blue's side.

'My fire's gone out. Care to light it?'

Conversation between him and the other men ceased. The bluest of eyes looked up at her and her legs went weak. She swallowed the impulse to sigh.

'Sure.'

His gaze held hers as he struck a match, then held it to the tip of her cigarette.

Holding his gaze with her own eyes, she covered his hand with hers, her fingers stroking the few hairs that lay darkly against his skin.

The intention was not lost on him. She saw the spark of interest in his eyes, and knew that in time she could make it become a flame.

'You're Blue Bonecci, right?'

Blue nodded.

'I'm Gloria Glammer.'

Blue laughed.

'No really. That's my name. G-L-A-M-M-E-R. That's how it's spelt. Suits me, don't you think?'

The other guys at the table began to laugh.

'That's what I like, a girl with glamour!' exclaimed one of them. 'I'm yours for the taking.'

Gloria ignored him. Her gaze was locked with that of Blue Bonecci. A slow smile was spreading across his face, and the corners of his eyes were crinkling in amusement.

'How about you, honey pie,' she simpered. 'Would you like a bit of Glammer?'

'Just a bit?' Dark eyebrows rose with sardonic amusement.

'One bit at a time, sweet thing. A little bit of this, and a little bit of that. My, my. Before you know it, you'd end up with the whole thing wouldn't you, honey pie? You greedy old thing, you!'

She chucked him under the chin and hunched her shoulders so that her nipples peeped over the low cut neckline of her dress.

'Steady now, honey,' he said, his eyes holding hers. 'You're just liable to tumble out of that dress you're almost wearing.'

'Oh, Mr Bonecci!' She patted his face, hunched her shoulders again, and turned to go, making sure her back was well hollowed, her buttocks prominent. Just as she had guessed, his hand landed a slap on her meaty behind. She squealed just as she was expected to, then looked over her shoulder coquettishly and into the smouldering eyes of Blue Bonecci's long-time girlfriend.

'Careful, Blue,' she heard Una say. 'That ass is big enough to bite!'

Gloria merely giggled as she wiggled away. Her smile stayed fixed, and she continued to laugh with the guys for the rest of the night, bubbling with happiness, and dancing for joy.

Inside she smouldered with excitement. Every so often she looked over at Blue's table, and every so often, she saw him looking back.

It was a few nights later when Una had supposedly gone to visit a sick relative that Blue came calling.

Gloria got back to her apartment in the early hours of the morning, and although Blue had sat watching her, she had not approached him. Instead, she had danced with all the most fanciable young men, laughing at their stupid jokes, and squealing as their youthful fingers had explored her body.

And all the time, Blue had watched, and all the time, Gloria had seen that spark of interest grow to a fierce flame.

Standing before a full-length mirror, she took off each piece of clothing until she stood only in silk stockings and pale blue garters. Pale blue and pale pink were her favourite colours. They suited her blonde hair and fair skin, and made her baby-blue eyes seem bluer, her cupid's bow mouth more innocent.

He'll call soon, she told herself as she stood admiring her full breasts and the sort of hips that Old Masters had painted in sunny Florence and sophisticated Paris.

The brass and green marble clock sitting on the mantelpiece struck the half hour past two when she heard the car draw up outside.

She peered through the flouncy-edged lace curtain. Below her were the gleaming lines of the yellow and chrome Studebaker belonging to Blue Bonecci.

Her hand flew to her breast as if she were half expecting the quickening beat of her heart to send it through her ribs.

'He's here,' she muttered with satisfaction.

She flew to the chair on which lay her blue silk wrap. Next, she bent one knee as she fiddled with her curls and sprayed fresh perfume around her neck, between her breasts and directly onto her pubic hair.

When the doorbell rang, she was ready for him. She untied the belt that held her wrap together, tousled her hair and practised the sleepy yawn of someone dragged from their sleep. Blue would be unable to resist her.

When she opened the door, it was Lenny, Blue's driver standing there. 'Sorry to wake you, ma'am.'

Hurriedly, she refastened her sash. 'What do you want? It's late,' she added.

'Sorry, ma'am. But the boss says I'm to fetch you right now. He wants you to come for a drive.'

'A drive? Sure, just wait while I get dressed.'

'No, ma'am.' Lenny's thick fingers wound around her wrist. 'He says right now, ma'am. As you are will do nicely for what he's got in mind.'

'My keys,' she cried, and briefly wondered whether her wanton behaviour earlier in the evening had upset him. If it had, his love-making might get pretty rough.

She slid her keys into her pocket, thankful that none of her neighbours were in the corridor at this time in the morning to see her gaping garment and the glimpses of naked breasts and bare belly.

Outside, the cool night air caressed her flesh and tickled her pubic hair. There was something exciting about being half naked and dragged along the sidewalk at the command of a man she desired. On the other hand, the fear that she might have offended him would not go away.

'Get in,' said Lenny as he opened the door.

As Gloria slid along the smooth leather seat, her silk wrap gaped and exposed her generous charms.

'Hi!' she said brightly and wriggled her fingers in a childish wave. Blue smiled, but his manner was oddly aloof.

'Drive!' he snapped. 'I've told you where.'

Gloria positively blossomed with dumb blonde vitality, but her fists were clenched tightly at her sides.

'I was in bed,' she cooed. 'All alone of course. Sound asleep. I wasn't expecting to be out sight-seeing at this time of night.' No trace of the panic she felt inside filtered through to her voice. At least, she didn't think it did.

'I am sight-seeing,' Blue returned.

Street lights intermittently lit the contours of his face. Gloria saw his smile and the look in his eyes. Slowly, like the rushing of sand from one glass bowl to another, her fear lessened. Only confirmation of his intentions would dissolve it completely.

'I'm cold,' she murmured at the same time as a powerful shiver ran through her body. 'Your driver didn't give me time enough to dress.'

One breast became completely exposed. Both nipples were in full view, although only noticeable with the aid of the passing street lights.

'Come here,' said Blue putting his arm round her and pulling her close. 'Let me warm you up.'

With his free hand, he covered her breast, his fingers spreading wide so as to fully encompass the ample flesh.

Expecting him to kiss her lips, Gloria tilted her head back, then gasped as the heat of his breath sent enticing thrills racing down her throat.

Teeth grated against skin. Tongue licked at flesh, lips sucked as if drawing out her life juices.

Low, guttural sounds that were half moans and half words of surprise poured from her mouth. Closing her eyes, she let the sensations he had aroused flood over her.

There no longer seemed to be any breath left in her throat. Her breast felt as if it were not made of flesh, but merely of sensations because his thumb, his fingers, and the palm of his hand had deemed it be so.

'Oh, baby! ' she squealed as his hand left her breast and squeezed her belly.

She fully expected his hand to go further, his fingers to tangle in the golden fleece that covered her pubic lips, but just as the car came to an abrupt halt, so did his hand.

'Let's walk,' he ordered.

Lenny opened the car door on her side. She slid along and got out, aware that the lights of the city were blinking in the distance, but not having a clue where they were.

'I like nature. Don't you?' Blue asked.

He was eyeing the dark trees that lined the rough road they had driven along. The sky overhead was still heavy with stars, and the air was warm.

'Are we far from Chicago?' Gloria asked.

'Far enough,' he answered. 'Come on. Let's walk.'

She started to do just that, when suddenly he stopped and pointed at her wrap.

'Take it off. It's a warm night.'

She complied, uncaring of the fact that it was Lenny who took the wrap from her, but hugely satisfied to see that both men were feasting their eyes on her body.

Half expecting him to put his arm round her again, Gloria began walking close to Blue's side.

'You sure are exciting,' she began, glancing at him and aching inside to see he was looking, not at her as she'd expected, but straight ahead. 'Are you always in the habit of—'

'Walk in front of me.' His command was sharp.

Uncompromising. 'I want to watch your ass as you walk.'

Forgetting herself for the moment, Gloria frowned and put her hands on her hips.

'Now look here, honey pie, I don't know . . .'

Blue stopped, grabbed her, and turned her round to face him. He placed his hands on her shoulders, and for the first time, Gloria felt the full power of his incredible charisma.

Ire melted, frown disappeared as his eyes looked into hers.

'Gloria Glammer, you have the most outstanding ass I have ever seen. Can you blame me for wanting to watch it in action?'

Gloria shivered. Flattery was the very life blood of her existence, especially when it was coming from the object of her desire. Her smile was instant and wide.

'If that's the sight you want to see honey, then that's the sight I'm going to show you!'

Hips swaying from side to side, buttocks moving in a provocative, rumba like action, Gloria sashayed away a few yards ahead of Blue.

Hands on hips, nipples hard as hazelnuts, she hummed a snatch of *Anything Goes*, sure now that Blue was within her grasp, and equally sure that her big, bouncing bottom was far and away her best asset.

Her flesh trembled in response to the night air on her skin, not because it was cold. On the contrary, the soft breeze that disturbed her pubic curls was warm. It caressed her back like long delicious fingers. Lightly, it kissed her nipples and swept over her buttocks like a swathe of soft silk.

Sensations normally only associated with the touch of another human being came easily into being, aided by the knowledge that Blue was walking behind her, watching as her right buttock rolled gently and provocatively against the left one.

How long, she thought, before he does it; before he can no longer resist the sight of it, but must have it. Must touch. Must . . .

The thoughts in her head became disjointed, replaced by the whirling heat of her own desire. Her flesh tingled as a faint flush started in the hollow between neck and breasts, then seeped like leaking ink all over her body.

Nakedness had become the most beautiful, the most warm of evening dresses. No sequined, tasselled creation of a Paris fashion house could ever equal it. Woman at her best should always be naked; like Eve, or Lady Godiva, or any of those Greek goddesses sculpted from stone; and each, she thought, looking completely unconcerned about it.

'Stop there,' Blue demanded.

She did stop. Her breath came in excited bursts. With the intuitiveness of a woman whose only talent is to appear submissive to a man, she did not turn round. Blue, she decided, would not want her to.

Even her breath seemed to tremble as he approached.

Only darkness lay ahead of her, yet she gazed at it as though it were the most glorious scene ever, because in her mind, it was. In her mind she did not see the trees. She only saw the rapture in Blue's eyes, could see his naked body and the stiffness of his penis as he approached her.

She gave a little gasp as his hand ran down her back.

'Lovely ass,' he said as he grasped one buttock then the other.

'Glad you like it, Blue, honey,' Gloria giggled. She turned her head, looked up at him over her shoulder, eyelids fluttering as if she were half afraid of seeing his expression.

'Like a horse,' Blue went on, his voice thoughtful as his hands caressed her behind.

'Oh!' Gloria said, not too sure the comparison was intended as a compliment or an insult. 'Whatever you say, Blue, honey.'

'That's it,' said Blue, sounding as though he hadn't really heard her. 'You can be my horse.'

'Well . . .' Gloria began, her voice uncertain and her giggle turning nervous. 'Blue, honey, I don't know . . .'

He took her chin between finger and thumb and turned her face up to look at him. 'You'll enjoy it,' he said, and kissed away her reservations.

'What are you doing?' she asked, and made a great effort not to sound nervous as she eyed the long silk scarves he must have carried with him.

'Put your hands up behind your neck,' he said, and because he kissed her again, she obeyed him willingly.

As he wound a silk scarf around her wrists, the response of her own body surprised her. Her nipples ached with desire, and that small nub of passion hiding between her legs, bristled as though it were no longer smooth, but covered in spines that grew and tickled the whole of her body.

Blue was playing a game she was none too sure of, and yet she could not stop him using her.

'Open your mouth,' he said.

He smiled as he said it, and his eyes sparkled in the light of the moon.

Mesmerised by the look and the smell of him, Gloria parted her lips and her teeth and felt the smoothness of the silk go into her mouth.

He knotted the scarf behind her head and threaded the long ends of it beneath her tied wrists.

'Now you are my horse,' he said, his voice thick with excitement. 'When I pull on the reins you stop, and when I do this . . .' Gloria yelped through the silk bridle as the end of something thin and sharp landed on her bottom.

'When I do this,' Blue went on, 'you get going.'

He did it again.

In her mind, Gloria wanted to rebel, but her body betrayed her. Her sex hung heavy between her legs, achingly submerged in the desire to please the male, to seep with sex juice, and do anything the man might want to do.

As the switch, or twig, or whatever landed for the third time, she leapt forward, her high heels wobbling at first as she fought to control her own confusion.

'Faster!'

Gloria's breasts jiggled as her buttocks responded to another lash. Awkwardly but quickly, she trotted forward, sweat running down her spine and between her breasts.

The ache between her legs intensified, and her muscles began to tremble. Her body felt as though it were no longer her own, but was being hijacked by the sensations flowing through her.

The secret nub between her sexual lips seemed to have developed a life of its own. Like a small porcupine, its spines moved as she moved, tickling her nerve ends, teasing her flesh towards a climax without the touch of human hand, but purely as a result of its own sexuality.

With the aid of his switch, Blue exhorted her to a run – an ungainly exercise on high-heeled shoes. As her pace quickened, so too did the onslaught of her climax. Her whole body trembled in one final act of betrayal. Silky fabric muffled her cry, yet Blue heard it.

As the last echoes of orgasm slipped silently from her body, Blue pulled her to a halt.

She stood for a while, trembling, sweating, and wondering what he would do now. His breath raced against her face. His hand cupped one buttock then the other.

'Well, that sure was a sight to behold,' he muttered.

Gloria gave a little cry as he squeezed her bottom. She wondered whether the switch had left marks. She also wondered what Blue would want her to do next and whether he would be annoyed about her having come before he had.

He eased the scarf away from her mouth and released her hands.

Breathlessly, Gloria regarded him, uncertain of what to say, what to do.

'Time we went,' he said, and began walking back to the car.

Gloria stood completely still, unsure of what had happened and what else was expected of her.

As though hypnotised, she watched him toss away the thin length of tree sapling with one hand, and stuff the silk scarves into his pocket with the other.

A terrible thought suddenly came to her. Was this it? Was he only going to take advantage of her this one time? That wasn't what she wanted. She wanted Blue, and she wanted everyone to know she was Blue's girl. If that meant playing his little games, then she would play them.

'Blue!' she called out suddenly. 'Wait for me, honey.'

Ungainly, naked, and tingling, she ran after him.

Blue got back to the car before she did. Unseen by her, him and Lenny exchanged a knowing look.

'A successful evening, Mr. Bonecci?' asked Lenny.

'Everything went according to plan,' Blue replied; then he turned and smiled as a breathless Gloria joined them.

Chapter 10

The waters of Lake Superior danced and sparkled gold in the late evening sunshine.

Three trucks with canvas-covered tilts sat near the water's edge, half hidden by the evening shadows thrown by a clutch of undergrowth and half a dozen dark-leaved spruce.

Their drivers and others sat on the front bumpers, caps pulled low over their eyes, ragged scarves pulled tight around their necks. Some read newspapers. Some smoked and narrowed their eyes at the glistening horizon.

'They're late!'

The man who said it got up and kicked at the dirt.

'I hate waiting around.'

'Relax. It's all part of the job,' said the one reading a paper. The cigarette that perched in the corner of his mouth did a jig as he spoke.

'Cut the talk.'

Ice strolled away from his lean, black Buick. The brim of his hat sat low on his brow so his face was half hidden in shadow.

'They're late,' repeated the guy who'd said it in the first place.

Ice glared at him, though not in the heat of anger. Even if he had been angry, the look in his eyes would still have been cold.

'They'll be here before the G-men.'

The man sprang to his feet. 'The Feds! Do you mean to tell me they know we're here?'

Ice turned his cool gaze to the sparkling water.

'The US has prohibition. Canada has distilleries. And the Great Lakes lie between us. Of course they know. Trouble is the shorelines of the lakes stretch for hundreds of miles. I'll lay bets of one hundred to one they'll never find us. Now relax. Be ready, and cut the conversation. Get it?'

Ice stared hard at the cloth-capped driver. The latter blinked, his knees buckling as the power of the former's gaze forced him to sit back down.

Once all was still and silent, Ice turned his eyes back to the lake, then skywards as a flock of geese flew in strict formation between him and the setting sun.

Shadows lengthened as the reddening sun settled closer to the horizon. Ice took a deep breath, revelling in the perfume of pine nuts and the crisp freshness of evening air.

It was, he remembered, on a night like this when he'd half carried Blue down a stony path through a clutch of dark pines and thick ferns.

As he remembered, a huge sigh seemed to pass through his heart as it had done many times after the night they had spent with the Indian girl in that simple log cabin.

Once the wild geese had passed, no sound remained except the rustling of the trees and the odd cry of wildfowl somewhere far out on the lake.

His thoughts would have stayed with that night high up in the Canadian wilderness if he hadn't heard the sound of a car approaching.

'Get down!'

As he dropped down behind his car, he signalled to the others. They all ducked down, their hands automatically going to their belts or pockets, gripping the deathly cold of hard metal, index fingers hovering over the trigger of a gun.

Ice gradually rose as two big headlights and the sleek lines of Blue Bonecci's Studebaker came into view.

Lenny was driving.

Blue got out, reached back into the car and pulled a thick overcoat out. Lenny helped him put it over his shoulders.

Ice kept his gaze steadfastly fixed on the boss as Una followed Blue out of the car, but he noticed exactly how she looked and his heart skipped a beat.

She was dressed in a dark blue suit trimmed with bright red. Her black hair lay sleek and glossy around her skull. Her eyes were like midnight, and her lips like newly spilt blood.

'Blue.' Ice nodded a cursory greeting at the boss. 'Una.' He nodded in the same manner at the boss's girl, but never allowed his eyes to stray in her direction.

For the briefest of moments, he thought of how easy it would be to take the colt from his pocket and aim it directly at Blue's heart, then to grab Una's hand, kiss her blood red lips, and seal their liaison by heaving her against the car, and ripping her dark blue clothes away from her creamy flesh.

'They're coming!' cried one of the drivers.

Reverie disturbed, Ice became instantly animated. 'Get

those trucks ready! Start the engines!'

'Good timing on my part,' chuckled Blue as he lit up a huge Havana.

Una leaned against the car as the men went to the shoreline, their forms sharply silhouetted against the gleaming orange and gold sky.

Along with the others, Ice screwed up his eyes as the incoming boats approached the shoreline. Ropes were thrown to the drivers and labourers so the motor launches could be pulled in as close as possible.

Speed and silence went hand in hand as box after box of Canadian Club was off loaded from the launches and reloaded onto the trucks.

'Blue!' shouted a man who wore no jacket and whose shirt was open to the waist.

Even as he leapt from the prow of a launch, his hand was already extended in greeting.

'McCloud!' cried Blue in response. 'The Captain Kidd of Canadian Club!'

They both slapped each other on the back, two men full of bonhomie and unsuppressed joviality.

'Ice!' exclaimed McCloud as he nodded at the others.

But Blue was the one who paid the green-backs, so he spent little time looking in Ice's direction.

'Watch those boxes!' Ice shouted as one man stumbled in the water. 'Break any of those bottles, and I'll be breaking your bones.'

His words were pure threat. Not only were the bottles nestled in heaps of close-packed straw, but the company had even replaced the familiar long-necked bottles with a short, stubby kind so breakages were kept to an absolute minimum.

Excused to oversee operations, he took the opportunity to glance in Una's direction. She was flicking cigarette ash off her breasts, and as she looked up, he saw her eyes flicker, knew she was looking at him and almost knew what she was thinking.

It had taken guts for her to be here, he reasoned. She knew that Blue was seeing Gloria, and although she had moved out from Blue's place and into a grim apartment on the wrong side of town, she had refused to leave the game entirely.

He wondered what her motives were; wondered at how hard it had been to swallow her pride.

But that should be no surprise, he told himself. Women did anything for Blue. Heart aching, he turned away. It was almost as though, he thought, women became poodles when Blue was around; performing poodles who would jump through hoops, stand on their hind legs and dance, or lie down and play dead if he wanted them to.

It was Blue Bonecci himself who interrupted his thoughts.

'Ice. I'm going back on the boat with McCloud.'

Excitement danced in Blue's eyes. Ice guessed at what McCloud might have suggested, but made no comment. 'You see this job through, will you. Tell Lenny to take the car and the broad home.'

Before the last case of spirits had been off-loaded, Blue's trousers were water-logged from the knees down. Ice noticed he kept the hem of his Kashmir coat clear of the lake.

'See you!' Blue called as the engines of the launch he

was on lurched into reverse. Blue waved briefly, then disappeared below decks.

'Alright!' Ice called as he turned towards the truck drivers. 'Get into your trucks and get going!'

Throbbing engine noises filled the air on both land and water.

Ice took a few steps backwards, his gaze thoughtful as the last truck pulled away and the last launch speeded over the water.

'Lenny,' he called without turning round. 'Take the car home.' He glanced briefly round, then kept his gaze fixed steadily on the water. 'I'll take Una home.' He could well imagine the look Lenny was giving him, and in order to avoid it, he kept his gaze firmly on the lake.

He heard the car engine thud into life and smelt Una's perfume as she came to stand beside him.

'Where's Blue gone?' Her voice reminded him of the sound of leaves rustling in a breeze.

'He's gone with McCloud.'

'Why?'

He sensed the tension just below the surface of her controlled exterior.

'Business.'

Judging by the look he'd seen in Blue's eyes, he knew that it wasn't the truth.

He felt Una's hand touch his arm.

'Do you believe that?'

He shrugged, aware that his heart was beating too fast and that he wanted to say much more than he should.

'It's what he said. Come on. I'll take you home.'

* * *

On the journey back to Chicago, a silence hung between them that was as deep and impenetrable as the oncoming night.

Ice could not resist glancing at her, keen to see the way the shadows of passing trees fell over her face. Just looking at her was usually enough to set his pulse racing, but the passing shadows cast an alarming spell that made him think her expression was altering, metamorphosing into someone or something he did not quite recognise.

'Blue's been seeing Gloria,' she blurted.

Her sudden comment made Ice grip the steering wheel that much more tightly.

'I know.'

He sensed her unhappiness, knew that tears were perched on the rims of her eyes.

'I suppose you think I'm mad to let him use me like he does.'

Ice shrugged. 'Your choice. Free country.'

Beneath his fingers, the steering wheel became Blue's neck as he gripped it more tightly.

She sighed and turned her gaze to the passing scene.

'Look at those trees. They remind me of home. I suppose I should have stayed among them. What do you think?'

Ice swallowed. The engine surged and he swerved slightly as his foot lunged too heavily at the gas.

'Like I said . . .'

'I know. My choice. It's a free country.'

It was gone midnight when they drew up outside the run-down building where Una now lived.

Ice switched off the engine.

'I'll see you inside.'

Una placed a hand on his arm. He could almost have believed it had burned through to his flesh.

'Don't!' she said. One word, yet to him it seemed like a statement of intent.

'I don't want to go to bed yet. I want to party. Will you take me to a club? Any club. Even one that doesn't serve booze.'

Her eyes looked up into his and the chip of ice that had been his heart pulsed with new life, new heat.

'OK.'

Although he drove with due care and attention, he wasn't really seeing anything. All he was aware of was that Una was sitting beside him, her hand was still on his arm and she had asked him to take her to a club.

This was the stuff of his dreams, of those sweet moments before waking when she lay naked in his arms, her bright red lips forming words of longing and love, her body undulating against his, his member dividing her sexual lips, moving gently, in-out-in-out.

He drove to The Palace Club; not a usual haunt, but one where only a few people would know him, and those not too sure of what he did or who he worked for.

'Is this a nice place?' Una asked him.

'I think we'll be OK here.'

'You mean Blue won't find out.'

He nodded and although he tried to fix her with his customary long, cool look, he felt himself blinking and an odd warmth spreading over his cheeks.

'It does food,' he added.

'Good.' Una got out of the car. 'I'm hungry.'

She slammed the car door, and with an affected jaunty air, glided towards the frontage of the club which more readily resembled a shop front than a palace.

Ice ordered steaks. He also ordered French claret, a taste he had acquired many years before he had come to Chicago.

'Would you like to taste the wine, sir?' asked the waiter.

Ice replied that he would.

Una, lips slightly parted, watched as Ice sipped at the glass and rolled the dark red fluid around his tongue.

'Perfect. Pour, please.'

'Certainly, sir.'

'I never knew you were an expert on wine.' Una sounded surprised and looked at him as though she'd never quite noticed him before.

'I'm not. I just know what I like.'

He realised his tone was curt, but he didn't want to go into aspects of his previous life. He wanted to hear her talk and watch the way her lips moved, the brightness of her eyes, and the way her breasts thrust forward with each sweet breath.

'Drink up,' he said. 'You'll like it too.'

She did as he suggested, rolling the liquid around her mouth then letting it settle on the back of her tongue before swallowing it.

'That way,' Ice informed her, 'you will taste every different aspect of the vintage, even down to the soil the vine was grown in.'

In a sudden moment of bravado, she drank the whole glass,

licking away the last red droplets from off her scarlet lips.

'Nice,' she exclaimed, and poured herself another.

Ice frowned. 'You're not going to get drunk, are you?'

Una smiled precociously, like some small, unpleasant girl.

'Why not? It's the fault of you men. You all drive me to drink.'

'Blue wouldn't like it.'

The moment the words were out of his mouth, he knew he'd said the wrong thing.

Una's eyes glittered. 'Fuck Blue! Fuck Gloria, and fuck you too!'

A few heads turned in their direction, but after a swift glance from Ice, looked away.

She drank that glass, then another. In between, she picked up her steak and bit into it, gorging on it like a starving dog would on a bone.

All the time, Ice watched, his frown deepening and his anger rising.

This was not the Una he had first met who had dealt with Blue's injuries, then taken both him and Ice to her bed. Had the big city really changed her that much, or was it her affair with Blue that had changed her?

His heart was heavy, and although he still felt some loyalty to Blue Bonecci, he also felt a great warmth for Una, and a great lust to have her body again.

There had only been that first time with both him and Blue. After that, she had become entirely Blue's property. Even the type of woman she had become was down to Blue's personal preference.

Not that he had a personal preference as such. He liked

all different kinds of women. It was just that the woman he had turned Una into was one of his imagination rather than flesh and blood. Perhaps because he couldn't find one like it, he had made Una in that image. And now look at her, he thought. Made into something she was not, and cast adrift.

Una began to shake her head from side to side like some rag doll that lacks stuffing around its neck.

'I want to drink. I want to be me again. I want to go home! I want . . . to . . . go . . . home!'

Before she crumpled to the floor, Ice paid the bill.

With his shoulder under her armpit, he heaved her to her feet and took her on unsteady legs, towards the door.

Other diners looked their way, but only to smirk and remark that yet another woman was no match for her drink.

As they drove to her place, her head lolled to one side and came to rest upon his shoulder.

The weight of it made his blood race through his veins. Any part of her body touching him immediately turned him on. Even one look from her was enough for that.

It was raining by the time they got back to her apartment. As they drew up outside, thin strips of rain whipped across the windscreen, then thickened and became heavier as the wind got fiercer.

Gently, he let her head settle on the seat, then went round to the passenger side, bent down, and let her flop over his shoulder.

He carried her upstairs like that, and after rummaging in her bag, gave up and butted his free shoulder against the fragile door.

It burst open easily, and he found himself in a room where

the dullness of the walls and furniture was only made bearable by the pink and blue of the neon light flashing just outside the window.

He let her fall onto the bed, and as her head hit the pillow, she moaned in a cat-like way that made him stop in his tracks.

There in the darkness, he stared down at her. The black bob that usually framed her face, was now spread around her head like the halo of some saint or angel. Her eyes were still closed.

Ice reached to turn on the bedside light, then thought better of it.

His thumb rubbed against the tip of his index finger as he looked at her, knowing what he wanted to do next, but also knowing what he should do.

Gently, unwilling to wake her, he undid the diamond shaped buckles of her shoes and slid them off her feet.

Once the shoes were off, he took hold of one foot and slowly pressed his thumb against each toe, starting with the biggest and working down to the smallest. As he massaged the toes of each foot, he pressed the palm of his hand against the soles of her feet so that her toes curled readily against his fingers.

He took her suit off next, the jacket first, then the skirt.

Even as he took them off, the smell of her body was already doing beautiful, sensual things to his own.

Her underwear was of cream satin. Thick bands of lace fastened the camisole top over her shoulders and edged the well-cut French knickers.

Ice licked at his lips. His eyes regarded the pinkness of her nipples which he could easily see through the flimsy top.

Raising her head gently from the pillow, he eased the top over her head. As he turned to place the top with her other clothes, he avoided looking at her naked breasts, unsure as to whether he could stop himself from ravishing her.

Slowly, he turned and let his gaze wander to her breasts. He sucked in his breath, and the ache that up until now had stayed in his heart, wandered down to his loins. He was stiff in his pants, and it frightened him.

As he stared at her breasts, he clenched his fists, curling his fingers into his palms. I mustn't, he thought. I mustn't.

Although his body ached with the sort of desire that made him want to rip her clothes from her body, he controlled himself. Taking deep breaths, he half closed his eyes, and once he was satisfied that he was again in control, he bent to her again and undid the buttons at the side of her knickers.

Sliding one hand beneath her back, he raised her slightly so the knickers slid over her thighs more easily.

Pink tipped breasts, a flat belly, a floss of jet black hair, and flesh touched with a creamy warmth he had never seen before now lay exposed to his gaze.

Unable to tear his gaze away from the sight of her, he reached behind him and let the silky underwear fall from his hand.

'Una.'

He said her name softly as if hardly daring to believe that such an ephemeral creature was real.

A few minutes passed, though it seemed to him like a lifetime. In his mind she was his and all the months she had spent with Blue were no more than the angry buzzing of a fly that stays just out of reach of a heavy hand.

Blue was losing interest in Una, yet was not quite ready to let her go completely. For a while she would teeter around the edge of him as though she were a Mayday dancer skipping around the Maypole at the end of a silk ribbon.

When, he wondered, would Blue let her go? When would Una realise the boss wasn't worth it?

Ice realised his mouth was dry, and the ache in his groin had become a pain.

Reverently, he reached for her, her nipple lengthening as his fingers caressed her breast.

She did not wake. Spurred on by his own desires, he caressed each breast in turn, his touch as light as a feather.

She murmured and arched her back. He thought he saw a smile of pleasure drift dreamily across her mouth.

'I can't help it,' he said softly, and sat down on the edge of the bed.

For what seemed to be an hour, but was no longer than a minute, he feasted his eyes on her breasts, her belly, and the perfect sweep of her thighs.

Touching her as if she were made from the most fragile of crystal, he ran his fingers over her breasts, trailed soft, exquisite lines down over her belly, then teased her pubic hair between his finger and thumb.

She stirred, but not with displeasure.

Suddenly, the ache in his groin was too much to bear, and what he saw of her body was no longer enough. Running his hand down her leg, he wound his fingers around her ankle and raised her foot to the height of his shoulder.

His breath caught in his throat. Before his eyes was her open slit, the inner flesh gleaming like pink satin, the outer lips luxuriant with black, sleek hair.

He ran his free hand down to his groin and felt the hardness of his cock. It jerked at his touch as if demanding to be set free.

'No,' Ice whispered. 'I can't.'

But the sight of her most secret place was too much for him to resist.

Adjusting himself on the bed, and still holding her leg high, he bent to her sex, smelt the femininity of her body, then kissed her mons, taking the hair into his mouth, tasting its saltiness, tasting the unique piquancy of her.

Her buttocks rose slightly from the bed, and he heard her moan. Yet she did not protest.

Sniffing her as though she were the most scented of flowers, he poked out his tongue and licked at her clitoris. He wrapped his tongue around it, prodding and pressing at it as if it were capable of dissolving in his mouth.

With his free hand, he unbuttoned his flies and let the hot, hard length of his prick fall into his hand.

As he licked at her sex, he wrapped his fingers around his prick and began to pull.

The tip of his tongue continued to explore the frilled flesh of her body, licking away all excess moisture, and delving into the dark opening of her vagina which glistened with more juice.

He sucked at her as he would at a slice of melon, the juice pouring over his chin as he fought to take the sweet flesh into his mouth.

Yet his tongue was gentle. He coaxed, but did not demand, caressed rather than prodded.

Like a small penis, his tongue entered her vagina, and at the same time, the vein running up the rear of his penis throbbed against his thumb.

Was it his imagination, or had he really felt her body tense, her buttocks quiver slightly as though some great force had been released inside her?

He couldn't be sure. Besides, he was so enamoured of the taste of her and his semen was rising quickly up through his stem.

A redness came to his mind, an explosion of light, scent, feelings, and incredible sensations.

His cock jerked in his hand, his semen spurting out of its end in long, milky globules.

Orgasm became a state of mind as well as a state of body. Its power was so all-enveloping, that he hardly noticed the shivering of her bottom, the new moistness of her sex.

With shame-filled eyes, he eyed the sticky white mass deposited on her bedspread.

'She mustn't know,' he uttered softly.

There was a small bathroom off to the right. Without switching the light on, he rummaged around until he found a wet face flannel and a dry bath sheet.

He covered her up before he left, tucking the bedclothes in around her as though she were a favourite child.

For a while, he watched her sleeping, her face pink now and shiny in the glare of the blinking neon outside the window.

Inside he felt elation, but also lost. How likely was it that he would taste her flesh again?

He didn't know, and that saddened him.

Eyes softened with affection, he looked at her one more time, his hand already on the door handle.

For a moment, he didn't stir.

'I think I love you,' he said softly. 'I really think I do.'

After he'd gone, Una opened her eyes very slowly and stared at the ceiling.

Up until now she had felt bitter that Blue had betrayed her, and angry that no one seemed to care. Suddenly, all that had changed. Ice cared. If she were clever she could use him to get back at Blue, till death if need be.

Death, she thought, and imagined Blue pleading for his life, begging for mercy at her hands as she smoked a cigarette through a holder, and Ice held a gun at his head.

She smiled. The scenario amused her.

She ran her hand down over her belly and let her finger dally between her thighs. Her hips jerked as the last waves of orgasm left her clitoris.

Ice, she decided, had more talents than she had realised, and the thought of him made her smile.

Chapter 11

Kitty Hawkins liked to think of herself as a mother figure.

Not that she was that much older than the girls she befriended, but she figured she had the experience they could learn by.

'You want to forget him. Blue Bonecci is a jerk. Leave him be.'

Gloria sobbed uncontrollably.

First Una, Kitty thought, now Gloria. How many more young women would the toughest mob boss in Chicago use then discard?

'But I want him!' Gloria wailed.

'That's a real problem for you, dear,' Kitty retorted, her tone more curt than it had been because, quite frankly, her patience was running out. 'You'll find someone else.'

'I don't want anyone else. I want to marry him.'

Kitty raised her eyebrows. 'Are you kidding?'

'Everything will be alright if we get married,' Gloria sobbed before sneezing into a blue silk handkerchief that Kitty had sewn from worn out underwear.

Kitty shook her head in disbelief and put the coffee pot down on a lace-lined tray that some aged aunt had given her.

Like the aunt, it had been formed before the Civil War and was looking past its best.

Fists clenched, Kitty stood with arms akimbo, a deep grimace on her face, and an equally deep frown on her brow.

'Marriage is not necessarily a cure-all. Most men get worse with familiarity in my experience.'

A tearful Gloria turned a pink, smudged face up to her, eyes big, blue and full of unshed tears.

'But how would you know? How *could* you know? Just tell me that!'

For a moment, Kitty was taken aback. Then she sighed and slowly lowered her slim bottom into a comfortable pale brown armchair. She clenched her jaw and hammered an equally clenched fist into a cushion before leaning back.

Memories of what had been and what might have been came back to haunt her, and as she considered them, she entwined five elegantly slim fingers of the right hand with five from the left around her knee.

'Experience,' she said softly as she rocked gently backwards and forwards in the chair. 'Put it all down to experience.'

Hair sticking in wet strands to her cheeks, Gloria dabbed at her eyes. She looked puzzled.

'What do you mean?'

Kitty looked away. 'I was married. Once. Just once. And that once was enough.'

Gloria sniffed. 'What happened?'

Kitty ran her fingers through her hair which was cut shorter than anyone else's.

She glanced quickly at Gloria before allowing herself the

luxury of talking about her hopes for her marriage and its failure.

'I thought I had the lot. He was a wealthy man, older than me, and I adored him.

'Do you know, my mother used to say to me, better to be an old man's darling than a young man's slave. Believe you me, there's no real difference. You can become a slave to an old man as easily as you can a young one. A lot of it is to do with them trying to regain the sensations they experienced in their youth. The trouble is those sensations need a lot more to get them going than when they were younger. That's how men become perverts.'

Gloria looked shocked. 'Is that what I was? A slave?' she asked.

Kitty looked away. There was a hint of the pain she herself felt in Gloria's eyes. It was like looking into a mirror, and it was far better for her own peace of mind to avoid looking at it.

'It didn't seem that way at first,' she said quietly, a smile softening the angular lines of her face and forgiving the thinness of her lips.

'You know how it is. Love grabs hold of you. Sex comes along with it and hijacks you into a fantasy world. Our love life was good when we first got married. Was for some time afterwards. We just couldn't get enough of each other. But you know how it is, palates become jaded and you want more of a kick, more of a buzz. Especially in the case of an older man.

'At first we tried it with other couples. Jack would screw the other woman, while her man screwed me. There we would be, all lying in the same bed, naked and glistening with sweat.

'It was good and I didn't complain. But I could see it wasn't enough for Jack. He wanted more. He wanted to try other things, darker things. I was game, after all I loved the guy and trusted him completely.

'Things progressed, and he told me one night he had a surprise for me. I was lying there in bed after drinking too much champagne. He told me I should be ashamed of myself and needed punishing. I just laughed.

'I thought that meant he was going to take me across his knee and spank me. He liked doing that and I liked him doing it. But this night was different.

'I was lying naked, face down and I laughed and pretended to struggle as he spread my legs and bound my ankles and wrists to the bed.

'He gagged me, and that was alright by me too. Then he smacked my bottom and called me a naughty girl. This was going to be a fun night, I thought. But suddenly I was aware that we were not alone.

'There was a big dark figure in the room. His shadow fell over me before I actually saw him. We'd played these sort of games before, but never with anyone else, and on this occasion, Jack had not told me that anyone else was coming.

'I felt nervous, but I trusted Jack. Perhaps I was going to have two guys at the same time. I had no quarrel with that. Gluttony is one of my worst sins believe it or not. I eat a lot, but I stay skinny because I screw a lot.

'Mind you, it surprised me when I saw Jack pull up a chair and sit himself down in it. Then I realised. Jack was going to watch. Perhaps, I thought, he would take his turn later on.

'I felt the stranger's hands run down my back.

'"She's got soft skin," he said. 'His voice was higher than I imagined it would be. Something about that unnerved me.

'"It'll still be soft when it's a little more pink," I heard Jack say.

'My heart jumped. There was now no doubt in my mind that I was going to get the switch or the strap across my body. Jack had done it before. It was just another game. My flesh would tingle nicely afterwards, and Jack would rub cream over me before falling asleep. Sometime later, he'd untie me.

'But never had a complete stranger done this to me. And with Jack watching!

'"Too much champagne, you say?" said the big dark man.

'"Too much champagne," Jack repeated. "She's always been a glutton. She needs to be punished."

'"I quite understand."

'I struggled a bit and made noises of protest, but I was gagged so they couldn't hear what I was saying. I shivered when his hands ran down my body and patted my behind.

'"Nice ass," he said.

'"I like it," said Jack.

'"She's had it there?" asked the dark man.

'"Sure," Jack replied.

'He was telling the truth. There were no holds barred between me and Jack. And anyway, we were husband and wife.' Kitty paused and sighed.

Gloria's mouth resembled that of a fish gasping for air.

Only it wasn't air she was gasping for. Listening to Kitty was better than reading a dirty passage from one of the European novels she was so fond of.

'What happened next?' Gloria asked. She eased herself from her chair and sat on the floor, her chin resting on Kitty's knee.

Kitty turned her cow-brown eyes on the girl, thought how pretty she was and inwardly smiled.

'Do you really want to hear, Gloria, darling?'

She ran her fingers through Gloria's hair, pushing the silken strands away from her glistening forehead.

Gloria nodded, her eyes bright with interest.

'OK.' Kitty nodded, and as she restarted her tale, she continued stroking Gloria's platinum head.

'"Has she had it lately?" asked the dark man.

'"Not lately," Jack replied. "I've been feeling a bit fed up with doing it myself. It becomes tedious. I'd like to see someone else do it."

'The dark man must have nodded. Anyway, some agreement was reached. I struggled as the stranger's hand went between my legs. His thumb pushed between my cheeks and he made me slick with cold cream.

'I remember thinking how hard his body was, and despite myself, I actually enjoyed what he did to me. As he did it, his hand was underneath me. That guy knew exactly what to touch and how to touch it to bring me off. My, but it was incredible. Especially with Jack sitting there watching.

'But that was the problem. Jack was none too pleased that not only had I come, but I had enjoyed it. You see what I mean about older men? Their tastes become perverted because they're losing it. He wanted to enjoy watching me squirm, not enjoying myself. Can you believe it?'

Gloria shook her head. Her mouth still hung open. Her eyes were wide with astonishment.

'Men!' Kitty spat the word. Then she leaned forward and cupped Gloria's face in her hands. 'We can do without them, honey.' She kissed Gloria's forehead. 'We can definitely do without them.' Her lips merely grazed Gloria's nose before fastening on her mouth.

At first she threw up her hands and pressed them on Kitty's shoulders, meaning to protest. But her tension vanished. Slowly, she wound her arms around Kitty's neck and stretched so she could more easily enjoy both the feel and the flavour of the other woman's lips.

Chapter 12

Danny Buller looked too sleek a man to have such an aggressive name. His trousers always had dead straight creases, his jackets were always buttoned, and his shirts were always stiffly starched and very white.

Judging by the way his jacket covered his body, no one could possibly have guessed that he wore a government-issue holster which held a government-issue pistol.

Although Blue Bonecci may not have remembered it, Danny Buller had grown up in the same neighbourhood, shared the same gang fights, and even the same girlfriends. Their paths had divided after leaving school.

Blue had chosen the wild side of life and a way of making a living that knew no laws and no morals.

Danny, dominated by a mother brought up as a Fitzpatrick in County Tipperary, had been bullied into graduating and, after a period at college, had ended up an officer in military intelligence. From there it had been a short skip and a jump to the Federal Bureau of Investigation.

But Danny had never forgotten Blue Bonecci, the good looking wop, loved by the girls and favoured by women who were old enough to know better.

At this very moment, Blue was in the car ahead of him.

'Don't lose him,' Danny growled.

John Benn, his driver, responded by stabbing his foot on the gas pedal. The car lurched into a higher speed.

'Do you think he's seen us?' John asked.

'Who cares!' Danny said, eyes narrowed and fixed like searchlights on the car in front. God, but he wanted to nail Bonecci. Any way, any which way at all. Vengeance was in his soul, yet he regretted it affecting his personality. 'Sorry, John. I didn't mean to be grouchy. It's just that me and this guy have got a score to settle. He probably does know we're following him. A guy in his position expects it.'

The car in front turned into an ill-lit side street.

'Pull in behind him,' Danny ordered.

Dark as the street was, Danny ground his teeth as he recognised the film star looks of the boy who'd been a class mate and had lived just a block or so away.

Like him, he'd been just this side of poverty, but unlike him, he had chosen a crooked path to follow.

Dishonesty wasn't the reason for Danny's hatred of the Italian mobster. There were plenty of them, and although he disliked them, they did not fire Danny with the same flame of revenge. Blue was someone he truly hated, because Blue was a man who used women and discarded them as if they were old shoes.

Danny's sister, Patsy, had been no more than sixteen when she had fallen for Blue.

Her hair was a fiery Irish red, and her eyes were green. Creamy skin and an infectious laugh had set her apart, above all the girls in school and all those in the neighbourhood.

She could have had the pick of any football jock, any high-brow swotter, any clever dick earmarked for Harvard or Yale. But she didn't fall for any of those. She fell for Blue.

Even when he had tired of her, she couldn't get over him. She'd followed him around, told him she'd do anything to have him back.

He'd laughed at that. Someone had told Danny so. Then an idea had come to Blue. He said he liked to share everything he had and she was no exception. Patsy had been stunned at first, but she was so besotted with him she'd have done anything.

Although they were not alone, he undressed her there and then. All the while, she had looked into his eyes as if mesmerised. Soon, she had stood naked, and his friends had gathered round. He'd told her to stand still as their hands explored her body. She'd trembled when he'd asked her to perform things with his friends. Each man to either side of her had taken his penis from his trousers. Blue had ordered her to take one in each hand.

'Give them some pleasure,' he had ordered. 'Go on. I want you to.'

She had done as he said. Not once had her eyes left his face. She was doing it for him, showing him just how much she loved him.

Things would have gone a lot further if Danny hadn't arrived. He'd wrapped his sister in his coat and grabbed her clothes.

Used to having his own way even if it meant using force, Blue had got angry. Eyes blazing, he'd leapt forward, his fists clenched.

But Danny wasn't some little Italian kid, bound by Mafia tradition and willing to submit to those more brutal than him. Defiant Irish blood had formed Danny into the man that he was. Four inches or more taller than Blue, he straightened to his full height and struck a blow with a fist that hit Blue between the eyes before the guy could possibly throw a punch at him.

But Patsy had never got over it, not in Danny's opinion. Why else would she have turned down all those doting young men and enrolled as a novice at the Convent of Our Sisters of Mercy?

His darling sister was beyond his reach, and Blue Bonecci was responsible.

Now he watched as Blue got out of the car and made his way into the Deep South Club. He noticed it was a different girl on his arm, another smiling, silly girl whom he made feel like a queen before treating her like a whore and shedding her like a snake sheds its skin. Another heart hurting.

In time, he thought to himself, Blue Bonecci would get his just rewards. He hoped he was the one to administer it, but inside he knew that the mob boss had made other enemies in his life, and their thirst for vengeance might be more pressing than his.

'Are we staying here long, boss?' John Benn asked.

'As long as it takes.'

John Benn folded his arms, pulled his hat down over his eyes and made himself comfortable.

'Could be a long night then.'

'Could be. Though I could always tell you a story.'

'What sort of story?'

'One that will make your toes curl.'

John laughed. 'How about one that makes my pant dog sit up and beg?'

'Now what do you think old J. Edgar H. would think of that?'

Considering how the boss of the FBI would react to the news that they were having erections whilst on duty made them burst out laughing. Hoover was known to be more fond of his mother than of women, though that could mean anything.

'I hear old J. Edgar never has an erection. Do you think he's got a pecker?' John asked, and sounded dead serious.

'Do you mean do I think he's a eunuch?'

John looked at him quizzically. 'What's that?'

Danny smiled and shook his head. 'Eunuch's have no balls. Some have no peckers either. The Turks, Arabs, and other Asians used to use them to guard the harem where their women lived. Poor bastards. Those without peckers had to pee through a straw.'

John looked at him in amazement. 'So they could never have a woman? That's tough!'

'Some could,' Danny replied. 'It depended on when they actually had them cut off. If they were half way or through puberty, then they could get an erection. These eunuchs were particularly popular with the women. They had no balls, so there was no fruit if you see what I mean. Handy, huh?'

John blinked like an owl surprised from a long sleep.

'I'd sooner be a monk than go through that.'

Danny nodded in the direction of the nightclub. 'At this

moment in time I'd like to hear what them three dames are saying.'

John Benn looked to where his boss was looking. Three women were watching Blue Bonecci's car from the other side of the street. They were half concealed by the shadows, but a stray beam of light had caused something metallic to glint sharply then disappear. Danny guessed it to be a gun. His instinct told him that these three women were not out to get Blue Bonecci's autograph.

Chapter 13

Covered only by a thin cotton sheet, Ice lay quite still, his eyes following Una's every move.

As on that very first night in this apartment, the only light was provided by the pink and blue flash of the neon just outside the window. He vaguely remembered it advertised some kind of powder for sprinkling on baby's bottoms, and thinking of pink, soft bottoms made him instantly think of Una.

The cool gaze of the man they called Ice followed the pert, firm bottom of the enigmatic Una as she slowly disrobed.

Ice sighed.

'Is something the matter?' Una asked, her voice as slow and smooth as honey.

Ice slowly shook his head. His gaze fastened on her small, round breasts and the delicious folds of flesh that appeared across her ribs and belly when she bent down to step out of her knickers.

'I was just thinking that watching you was better than going to the movies. It's more interesting. More exciting.'

She lowered her eyelids and he thought he detected a faint

blush on her cheeks as her cherry red mouth smiled.

When she was completely naked, she got onto the bed, her knees astride his legs, her hands beside his head and her breasts within kissing distance of his mouth. He lay his hands palms upwards and let them rise until her nipples were settled spot in the middle of them.

It seemed too long a time before her face was near to his, her lips kissing, her hair tickling his cheeks.

Clasping her breasts, he pulled her closer, then ran his hands round her back and held her tightly against him.

Closing his eyes made her presence seem more intense, more sexually overpowering than when they were open. It also shut out the drab decor of the room and the sickly light of the flickering neon.

The sheet remained between their bodies, but was unimportant. Every contour of her body was etched on his mind. He could make love to her in his sleep or completely blind if he wished to. He knew her so well, slept with her even when they were apart.

She rubbed herself against him so that his shaft was adjacent to her most sensitive part. Little sounds of delight echoed against his ear as her cheek nestled against his.

Clasping her buttocks, he brought her hips further up his body, and as he did so, they both kicked at the sheet so that flesh met hotly against flesh.

She slid herself onto him so smoothly, so quickly, that he caught his breath, sighing with delight as she began to ride him, her buttocks soft against his thighs, the crispness of her pubic hair mingling with his.

Locking her elbows, she hovered over him so that he could

play with her breasts at will, grasping them, kneading them, tweaking her nipples and rubbing one firm mound against the other.

Her belly caressed his as she moved herself up and down on his shaft, taking it slow, then quickening the pace, the insides of her splayed thighs soft against his.

Placing both hands on her rib cage, he took some control of the action, using all his strength to push her down on his shaft before pulling her back up again.

The urge to see her expression was stronger than his wish to blot out the drabness of the room. His lover's eyes were closed, her head erect, and her mouth open. Her breath was quickening along with the action of her open thighs. He felt the soft sponginess of her flesh tightening around his penis, sucking at him like plump, succulent lips that are ravenous to receive the nectar he would offer.

Above him, Una shuddered and sighed, a long drawn-out sob leaving her lips as her hips tensed and her fleshy lips gorged on his semen.

They lay together afterwards, his hands caressing her back, always moving, always seeking the most tantalising spot.

He could tell which ones they were, because she would cease talking and mew like a kitten, or her back would arch, and one leg would rub languorously against the other.

One fear occupied Ice's head. So far he had not voiced it. He did not want to frighten her, and he had no wish to spoil the moment.

He had been loyal to Blue for a good while, and had known him for a long time. But there were limits. He realised that now.

115

A stronger force than loyalty now lay in silken knots around his heart. There was no wish in him to dominate Una and control her like some men felt it their right to do. He had a yearning to protect her, to have her close to him and feel them becoming one with the passing of the years.

'He'll kill us if he ever finds out.'

His words sent a chill through the air.

Una tensed, and he held her closer.

'We'll go away.'

'He'll find us.'

'Would he really kill us? I mean, he doesn't want me any more.'

'He hasn't cast you off entirely. He still picks you up and puts you down again.'

Una didn't answer. He sensed her pain, knew he'd spoken the truth, and also knew she was powerless to resist Blue. That's the way Blue was. Only when you were completely discarded were you free to make a life for yourself.

Suddenly, all the bitterness he'd stored up since finding Una in that log cabin came pouring over him.

If he'd made a play for Una then, he was sure she'd have been his girl, not Blue's. But he hadn't and he called himself a coward for not doing so.

'Blue's in Miami at the moment. He's got that new dame with him.'

'Gloria?'

'No. She's past meat. Amy. Yes. Her name's Amy.'

There was silence. Both were plotting, and when Ice spoke, he was only confirming what was in Una's head.

'We'll go. We'll make a break for it right now. Have you got your things?'

Una raised herself onto her elbows and looked lovingly into his eyes.

'I've got everything I need. Have you?'

He nodded.

By dawn they were nearing the Canadian border.

They were tired, thirsty and hungry when they pulled to a halt outside a ramshackle place that advertised Cola and best steak for forty miles. It was optimistically named The Gold Strike Motel.

'I'm tired,' Una said. 'How about a bed?'

Ice nodded. 'Just what I had in mind.'

He couldn't help putting a protective arm around her as they opened the squeaking door to the shabby reception. Protecting her might have been his main priority, but touching her automatically made him want her. He would always want her, he thought. Right up until the day he died. Thinking like that surprised him, but left him feeling warm.

Una slammed her palm down on the reception bell.

'Perhaps we're waking them.'

'Perhaps we're not,' Una retorted.

A string and bead curtain with twenty-five percent of its constitution missing rattled as a thick, red hand pushed it aside.

'Take your time,' said Ice.

The man looked like a lumberjack and had a black beard and piercing blue eyes. His tone was abrupt, though not exactly unfriendly.

Una gathered her dark green coat around herself that bit more tightly as his eyes raked her from head to toe, taking plenty of notice of the bit between neck and knees.

'What do you want?' He directed the question at her. At the same time, he chewed a match stick at the side of his mouth.

'I think we should go.'

Ice took hold of Una's arm.

'Don't do that.'

The unmistakable click of a safety catch coming off a trigger ricocheted around the room. There was a mad gleam in the man's eyes.

'You want money?' Ice reached into his inside jacket pocket meaning to pull out a lot more than his wallet.

The sound of the door squealing behind him was the last sound he heard before the butt of a shotgun crashed down on his skull.

Chapter 14

Ice shook his head as he came to. The room he was in appeared to be made of rubber because the walls, floor and ceiling kept wobbling and reshaping themselves. Gradually, his vision cleared, and when it did, he wished he was unconscious again.

Whoever had fashioned this room was into torture in a big way. There were iron cages, cat o' nine tails hanging from the walls, various harnesses and bridles that looked more suited to humans than horses.

Ice had heard of this sort of thing, though perversion of that kind had never interested him personally.

Because he knew there were people who did like that sort of thing, and because his mind was still a little groggy and therefore not entirely logical, fear did not overwhelm him – until he saw Una.

Her sleek, beautiful body was stretched out from ceiling to floor before his eyes. She was naked and her hands were tied high above her head. Thick manacles chained her ankles to the floor.

Two big guys, one of whom he recognised from the motel reception, stood next to her. Both seemed to be slobbering like huge rabid dogs as their eyes ran over her lean, smooth flesh.

In other circumstances Ice might have been turned on by it. But fear overwhelmed any sexual response he might have had.

'Una!'

The called name was nothing but a muffled mumble against the piece of rough cloth that gagged his mouth. It tasted of linseed oil and stale coffee and made him retch, a small discomfort compared to what Una was experiencing.

He clenched his fists and flexed his muscles in an effort to test the strength of his bonds. He just had to escape. He had to save Una!

'So you've got me naked and tied up. What next?'

Ice couldn't believe what he was hearing. Some women would have been crying or hysterical by now. Una was as cool as ice. At first it surprised him, then he realised it shouldn't. After all, hadn't they defied Blue Bonecci, the most powerful hood in Chicago?

Clever girl, he thought. Keep alert. Keep your wits about you.

'We're going to let you hang around here for a while. Me and my brother like to take our time.'

Both the big, black-bearded fellows laughed as one rubbed his round, clothed belly against her naked one, and the other rubbed his against her back.

'Nice tits, Abe,' said the first brother, the one who they'd met in reception.

Ice saw Una grit her teeth as a huge hand squeezed one pretty breast, pulling on it as though there were no human being attached to the other end.

'Nice ass,' the other guy commented.

Ice was stunned by the way Una remained silent and as still as she could as two huge thumbs divided her buttocks and pressed against the tight knot between them.

'Never mind, honey. You won't have long to wait,' said the guy who had squeezed her breasts, laughing. 'Be patient, honey. You'll have more than you can manage. We'll start with one of us going in frontwards, and one behind. Then we'll both have your mouth, and then we'll take it from there. And all the time, your boyfriend there will be watching.'

'Oh really?' Una's expression was as pert as her voice. 'So you two are the sort of guys who need to tie a woman up before they can get a hard-on.'

Una sounded real sassy. Ice wondered at just how brave a girl she was, or just how headstrong. Either way, she certainly wasn't acting as if sexual bullies could intimidate her.

The bigger guy grabbed hold of her face in his big hand and brought his ugly mug close to her face.

'Me and my brother Zeke will fuck you as you've never been fucked before, and each time Zeke finishes, I'll fuck you. And each time I finish, Zeke will be ready again. In time you'll be so full of our spunk, it'll be coming out of your mouth and running down your nose. So be patient, honey, and once we're back from taking our Mom shopping, we'll be here to give you our full attention!'

They laughed as they went, both of them slapping her bottom before leaving and throwing a lecherous, evil look in the direction of Ice, their bound and gagged captive.

A cloud of dust blew up from the floor as the door slammed behind them.

Una turned her eyes in Ice's direction.

'Can you move?'

Ice wriggled furiously, the rope cutting into his wrists, the gag straining against his mouth.

Una's sigh was not short of a heart-broken sob. She had been brave enough face to face with her captors. Now she had full knowledge of their intentions, she was terrified and close to breaking point.

'Please, Ice. You have to do something. You have to!'

Seeing and hearing her like that gave greater impetus to his efforts.

Although he felt blood trickle warmly down his wrists, he persevered, gritting his teeth behind the coarse cloth that gagged his mouth as he concentrated all his strength into getting away.

Whoever had tied him up was no sailor. The knots he used were slack, the sort intended for a horse so it doesn't strangle him if he jerks his head away.

Once his hands were free, Ice tore the gag from his mouth and gasped for air.

'Ice!' Una sounded ecstatic.

Ice tore at the rope that bound his feet. Then he was up and across the room in six long strides.

She shivered as he pulled her tightly against him.

'Ice,' Una murmured, her face buried against his neck as his lips kissed her hair.

'It's OK, baby. It's OK.'

But he wasn't entirely sure that they were.

Quickly, he searched in his pockets just to make sure that they had discovered and purloined his weapon. They had.

As he cuddled Una, he unlocked the manacles. Their captors had been arrogant enough to leave the keys in the locks.

All the time, he listened intently, his eyes searching the room for a possible weapon, but also in case a shadow fell through the cracked glass of the door.

'Delicious,' he heard Una murmur. 'Don't untie me just yet. Do it to me. Like this. Just as we are.'

Ice frowned as he looked into her face and was amazed to see her eyes were glittering and her plum red lips were parted and her tongue was darting in and out like a cobra about to strike.

Still with her arms fastened above her head, her body undulated against his, her breasts pressing against his chest, the nakedness of her belly against his groin.

To his own amazement, he felt his penis rising in his pants like a hound that has just got scent of the prey.

He smelt her scent, the odour of her sexuality filling his head and making him forget that they were in danger, that their captors could come back at any moment.

'Fuck me,' she said, her voice long, low and saturated with sexuality.

Despite his fears and his deep-rooted instinct to flee, he ran his hands down her back, feeling the tight nodules of her spine, the rise of her buttocks, the way they curved to the top of her legs.

Once he had felt her, there was no turning back. He had to follow the sweep of her hips, the swell of her belly. He had to run his fingers through the silky strength of her pubic hairs and delve into the succulent juiciness between.

What he found there amazed him further. Una was soaking wet and that hard nub usually so well hidden by her sexual lips, was hard, thrusting and jerking slightly against his fingertip.

'Now,' she pleaded as her hips gyrated against him.

Ice desired Una more than any woman he had ever known, and being no different than any other man, he could not ignore her demands no matter what danger they were in.

Besides that, the fact that she was helpless in his hands fired up his own libido. Now he was not only a victim of her demands, but a victim of his own passion.

His cock was swollen and ready to come out of his trousers. Before inserting it in her vagina, he ran it along the soaking lips of her sex, feeling the waves of flesh divide as he surged towards his goal.

Una was almost swinging on her chains as the thickness of his erection slid into her.

There were no words in the sounds she made. She closed her eyes and let her head loll away from him. Like him she had become the slave of her own sex drive.

'Delicious,' she murmured, her voice sounding small and far away. 'So delicious.'

His hands worked with serious precision either side of her spine and slid slowly to cover the rising mounds of Una's behind.

He saw her lashes flicker, her nostrils flare slightly and knew that Una's time was coming. Her orgasm was near, and so was his.

He detected a delicious shiver running down her spine. His fingers followed it, his hands gripping her behind as she purred against his ear and wriggled her pelvis against his.

As the most powerful shiver of all ran over her flesh, Ice held himself still until he was sure she was entirely spent. With one long, deep thrust, he let himself go. He had the odd sensation that his penis was covered in a velvet glove that caressed without fingers and spread its feelings of ecstasy all over his body.

They stayed tightly together, her naked and manacled, him fully clothed, his thoughts turning to the problems of getting away from here.

'We have to go.'

His movements quickened.

Once she was free, Una searched for her clothes. All she found were a pair of janitors overalls and a checked shirt. Both looked clean, as if someone's mother had lovingly washed and pressed them ready for her darling boy to put on.

'They'll have to do,' she said, chuckling when she saw the look on his face. She rolled up the legs and fixed the straps as high as she could so that the bib rubbed against her neck. The crotch came somewhere near her own, but not near enough.

Barefoot, and with Ice holding her hand, they made for the door. Ice peered out across the gravel yard, past the sign saying *Hot and Cold Running Water*, and a more down-at-heel one saying *Mom's Yummy Burgers*. Yuk!

Just as Ice was about to open the door, a cloud of dust

preceded the arrival of a pick-up truck whose paintwork might have been green, but could just as easily have been blue. Patches of rust connected the two colours.

'Get back.'

Ice pushed her behind him as he edged back into the room. Then he spun away from her, his eyes searching again for some weapon that would at least keep the two brothers at bay – even if it meant him holding them off while Una got away.

The cat was pulled from the wall. A long spear with a slightly African look about it, also looked pretty useful.

Once fully armed, Ice stood behind the door. Una leaned against the wall directly opposite it.

The two brothers laughed as they slammed the pick up's doors and sauntered across the gravel.

Una and Ice exchanged looks. Una broke it first.

'They might guess you're there!'

She was right. 'Then attract their attention!'

Una looked down at herself. She didn't look too attractive in the baggy clothes, but could do pretty well as a scarecrow.

With trembling hands, she undid the tight buckles a little, pulled the check shirt open, and pulled her breasts up over the bib. Ice saw what she had done and gasped.

'I didn't tell you to do something to attract *my* attention.'

'Good. If it attracts yours, it'll attract theirs!'

She was right. The tough cotton ridge of the bib held her breasts high. They looked more round, more obvious, and a lot more lewd.

When the door swung open, the brothers' mouths dropped to their chests. For just a few seconds, they were completely disarmed, their attention fixed on her exposed flesh. Before they could fully appraise the situation, the spear was through one brother's neck. He squealed like a wounded animal, his legs kicking, as Ice levered on the six-foot weapon.

So quickly did Ice move that then other man was transfixed, blood from his brother's jugular pumping over his hands as he tried to help him.

But Ice was free. The metal-plated ends of the cat wrapped round the man's head, one piece whipping across his eyes and leaving blood where an eyeball should have been.

'Run!' Ice shouted to Una.

Una dashed for the door, her bare feet leaving footprints in the pooling blood.

Sure now that his adversaries were incapable of hurting either him or the woman he loved, Ice shoved his hands into the pockets of their denim overalls. Just as he had supposed, one of them had his gun and the same one had his wallet.

'Ice!'

He turned to follow Una. The brother who now had a hole where an eye used to be, lumbered towards him. But Ice was quicker and more experienced in street fighting than this man could ever hope to be.

He ran out behind her, constantly turning in case by some miracle one of the brothers had got free and was foolish enough to follow.

The pick-up started on the third try, soon enough to get them away, off down the dusty road.

Their hearts raced as they drove. Una began to relax. Ice was in turmoil. Something about the whole scene had stayed with him, and he knew instantly what it was.

He had enjoyed what he'd done. A sense of pride had rushed through him because he'd saved his lady love from someone who would have abused her. It felt good, and because it felt good and because he was in love, a plan began to form in his mind.

He glanced at the young woman sat beside him who still looked good despite being dressed in such an unflattering uniform.

How would she react to the plan that was forming in his mind?

'Are you alright?' he asked.

'I am now. Those two were definitely not my type.'

Ice paused, unsure whether he should ask the next question, but determined to sound her out on what he had in mind.

'Was Blue really your type?'

He sensed her freezing.

'I thought he was at the time.'

But not now, Ice thought.

'He treated you bad.'

'He treats all women bad. In fact, he shames them.'

Ice smiled. 'Perhaps it's time a woman treated him bad. Perhaps it's time he was used like he uses and abuses them.'

He glanced at her face, saw the sudden lightening of her expression and how talking about Blue had darkened it again.

'Or perhaps more than one woman should use and abuse him,' he said.

Chapter 15

Rosa Bonecci raised her warm brown eyes to the altar and fingered her rosary as if she really were worshipping the effigy of ivory, silver and wood that was hanging there.

The cool dimness of St Mary's, the smell of incense, and the gleam of polished floors and wood touched by candlelight all assisted meditation. And Rosa was indeed meditating, not on religion, but on the behaviour of her son and her wishes for his future.

A small hand crept into hers. 'Will it be long?' Maria, her youngest daughter, whispered.

'Be quiet, child. You are in a house of God,' Rosa whispered back.

Although she appeared not to notice the few other people waiting to enter the confessional, she counted every creak of the small wooden door, and every set of footsteps that advanced then retreated away from it.

When her turn came, she was quick on her feet, heart pounding as she considered what she would say and how he would receive it.

'Stay here,' she ordered her small daughter, the fruit of her later years.

A man glanced at her as she went by, looked away, then glanced again.

Amazing. She was fifty-six years old, but still drew admiration.

The wooden door creaked again as she closed it and settled herself down on the small bench inside.

'It's me,' she said softly.

There was a pause, just as she expected there to be. Just as there always was when she came to confession.

'Rosa. How are you?'

'I'm well enough.'

'And how is Maria?' He said the words softly, almost reverently. Rosa smiled.

'She is growing more beautiful every day. She is like an angel.'

'Good.' There was another pause. 'Do you wish to confess?'

'I came for your help. I want you to speak to Bernardo.' She never could quite get round to finishing her sentence with 'Father' as a priest should be called. Sean was his name and that was how she always thought of him. Sean. Not Father O'Flanagan.

She heard him sigh.

'What can I say to him, Rosa? He has chosen the crooked path in life. I have already pointed out to him that it could lead to prison or the gas chair, but he just tells me to mind my own business, then gives me money for charity.'

'It's not that,' Rosa interrupted. 'Women are his problem. He has so many, and I think he should marry. If he has a wife and children, then perhaps he would not have so many others.' She paused. She knew her son well, as did the Roman Catholic priest sitting the other side of the fretwork partition. 'His appetite would not be so vigorous,' she finished. 'I would not expect him never to commit adultery, but I feel a wife could help. After all, none of us are without sin, are we?'

'I see.' He sounded thoughtful. She knew her last comment had sunk in.

'I'll speak to him,' he added.

'Thank you. Thank you, Sean. God bless you.'

He should have responded before he heard the door squeak open and knew she had left. But her visit caused Father Sean O'Flanagan to sigh and sink back against the warm wood, close his eyes and think of things long past.

Rosa had spoken little English when she had first come to confession. Like a lot of other girls from the old country, her marriage had resulted from family commitment, based on youthful attraction and expected to result in a good partnership.

Things had not turned out quite that way. Rosa had been a young woman in a strange country, incarcerated at home with two sons, and expected to keep house as though she were still in the old country.

But Rosa had been lonely.

Coming to confession became a thrice weekly occurrence. Confession had turned to conversations in the vestry, walks around the church when Sean had helped her improve her English.

In time, he had realised that his relationship with her was far more than just that of a priest and one of his flock. He had grown fond of her. In dreams that he had never expected to have again, the liquid warmth of her velvet brown eyes were looking up at him, her body was naked beneath his, his own pelvis were jerking up and down on hers.

Each morning after such dreams, he had risen early from his bed in order to strip the sheets lest his housekeeper see the stain stiffening the pure white cotton.

He had tried praying, fasting, even a bout of flagellation over his naked back, but no amount of penance quelled either the ache in his heart or in his loins.

In a crisp Autumn, when the wind was chill but the sky was blue and the sun shed its last golden rays before winter, their relationship had blossomed.

Rosa had just finished arranging flowers and sheaves of imitation corn and fresh fruit around the church, fitting decorations for that time of year. She was using the small sink just off the room where Father O'Flanagan kept the robes he used for ceremonial occasions along with spare hymn books, bibles, and the cloths and silver polish that kept the altar pieces bright and shining.

There was a door between the room and the washroom. Rosa had her back turned to him as he entered, the door half closed.

Dreams had yet again haunted his mind the previous evening, and Father O'Flanagan was feeling exhausted, his eyes red-rimmed, and his mind troubled.

He threw his head back and closed his eyes. 'Rosa! Rosa!' he called softly. 'Why do you tempt me like you do?'

Rosa had already been aware of him entering, but had not declared her presence. Like him, she was troubled. Wasn't it wicked to lust after a priest? In fact, she reminded herself, it is a sin to lust after any man. You are a married woman with two children.

But self respect was no match for the powerful feelings that started somewhere deep down in her loins and spread like wildfire throughout her body. As quietly as she could, she turned, pushed gently at the door, and stood there staring at him.

He blinked when he first saw her. Each gazed at the other as the whole truth became apparent. Despite his priestly vows, Father Sean O'Flanagan was a victim of his own chemistry, a pattern laid down in him at conception. And Rosa Bonecci was a victim of hers. They both wanted each other, and no rule made by either man or God was going to stop them.

Because he had been about to disrobe, Father O'Flanagan had bolted the outer door. Not that he would have thought of that at this moment. He and Rosa fell into each other's arms.

He rained kisses over her face, hardly believing that this was real and no longer a dream. He closed his eyes, then opened them quickly. She was still there, and he could feel her body and not just the stiffly starched sheets of a single bed.

Like a man that has been lost for weeks in the desert, he gulped at her, tore at her clothes and feasted his mouth on her flesh, sucked on her breasts, and hugged her warmth tightly to him.

She was like a new world to him, a land of peaks and troughs, dark valleys and rounded hills.

His fingers, palms and mouth explored her. He bent his head, took the swollen nipples into his mouth, and sucked on them, nipping them slightly so that they grew and became red and rosy.

Naked, they had lain on the vast wooden chest that held his vestments, and he had taken her there, his penis sliding into her with as much wonder as when Adam had first taken Eve.

This was heavenly, he thought. This was God-given – who was the fool who said a man must be celibate in order to see God? Nature, he realised, could not and would not be ignored. The power of attraction was seated in generations of procreation just as originally laid down in the book of Genesis.

God created Adam, and then created Eve and they were good.

Yes, he thought as truly mind shattering sensations exploded from his loins and racked his body, *Yes! This is good. And God created it.*

Rosa invited him to dinner on the pretext of discussing the details of Maria's confirmation. Blue had agreed to attend because he always made a point of dining with the family once a month. Tony, his younger brother, would also be there.

After eating a bowl of spaghetti that dripped with cheese and was served with a well-oiled salad, black olives and bread whose crust was still dusty with flour, Father O'Flanagan spoke with the men whilst Rosa and Maria cleared the table.

'This family is growing up fast,' he said casually as little

Maria threw him a big-toothed smile. He blinked quickly then looked away.

'It has grown as much as it's going to as far as I'm concerned,' stated Rosa's husband, his braces straining against the pressure of his waistline. 'No more children for me. I'm too old, besides, I can't take any more surprises. Maria was more than enough of one for me.'

The three male members of the Bonecci family laughed. The priest merely smiled quietly whilst his fingers played with a fork that had been left behind on the table.

'A task for the next generation,' he said and eyed the two brothers.

Blue's eyes met him head on. 'Are you trying to say that I should go forth and multiply, father?'

He grinned as he said it, but Father O'Flanagan instinctively knew that Blue was fully aware of his mother's intentions.

'Grandchildren would be nice,' said Blue's father, and looked as though he meant it.

'I wouldn't mind having children,' Tony stated, then paused. 'But I'd have to find a wife first.'

Blue laughed. 'Obviously. Otherwise our dear Father O'Flanagan will boast of the Bonecci family having a male Madonna. Just think of it, an immaculate conception in the Bonecci family!'

Tony laughed. Father O'Flanagan merely shook his head, and although he thought amusement at such a joke might be considered blasphemous, he could not suppress a weak smile.

Chapter 16

Ice found it difficult at first to put all that he was feeling into words. But Una listened, and as she listened her eyes sparkled and her sweet lips smiled.

'We're talking revenge,' she said blithely, and he knew her mind was walking the same path as his.

'I should kill him,' he said.

Una's smile disappeared. She laid her hand upon his arm. 'No. You mustn't. This is women's work.'

He frowned. 'What do you mean, women's work?'

Her smile returned and made him feel warm. Even if he'd been sitting there with no clothes on at all, she would still have made him feel warm.

She explained: 'Blue has never abused you. You're a lifetime buddy. Besides having the same three piece suite between your legs as he's got.' Her smile became wicked. She leaned closer beside him in the car and rubbed her hand over his crotch. 'But yours is nicer,' she murmured, and somehow he knew he wasn't being vain when he believed that she meant it.

Una patted him gently, then leaned back against the warm leather of the car seat. She began to chew thoughtfully at

137

her thumb: like a little girl, he thought, and knew he loved her.

'I said this was women's work,' she said suddenly. 'But we might need your help.'

He felt her looking at him and turned to look at her. She winked.

'Blue Bonecci is about to get his just desserts.'

He laughed because her smile made him feel happy, but there was a nagging doubt in his mind that whatever she was planning might be too dangerous. Blue Bonecci loved women, but not enemies, no matter what their sex.

It was dark when they got back to the city. Lights were twinkling from signs advertising everything from corn cures to boot polish. Suddenly, they seemed to be of great interest to his passenger. She studied them all, or was it the dark buildings on which they were fixed?

Ice pressed his foot on the gas. Somehow, he wanted to get her away from the bright lights, take her into his apartment and close the door on Blue and the city. He wanted to see her in a soft light, her silk underwear falling silently from her body.

Let it be white underwear, he thought. And let it be satin. Satin catches the light; looks alive. Like her. He thought of her breasts, of burying his nose between them, sniffing at her as if she were a highly perfumed rose. If he really concentrated, he could almost feel her flesh against his cheeks.

As they passed into clubland, where speakeasies were behind every darkened door, and the floor shows could be anything from jazz musicians to the most blatant of sex shows, Una suddenly held up her hand and asked Ice to pull over.

'What's that place there?' she asked.

Ice shrugged away his fantasies and his uncertainty. 'An empty warehouse?'

'It would sure make a pretty swell speakeasy,' Una murmured. 'Or a nightclub. A very special nightclub.'

Ice felt a shiver of apprehension cruise down his spine.

'You don't mean that?'

'Of course I do! My idea is to open a nightclub run purely by women.' She laughed. 'Just imagine the stir that would cause!'

Ice did, and immediately had an inkling of what might be in her mind. He wrapped his hand over her shoulder.

'Una. You can't do that. You know Blue has to give the OK to schemes like that. And he certainly won't give it to you.'

The defiant look she gave him made him wince.

'This sort of speakeasy won't be requiring his blessing, Ice, baby. This sort of speakeasy won't be serving booze like the stuff he sells. The floor show will be the main attraction, and once he knows about it, he won't be able to resist what it has to offer.'

'So what drinks will you serve? Tea? Coffee?'

'Champagne.' She laughed. 'Just champagne.'

Ice had serious misgivings about her plans. It was still in his head that it might be best to shoot his rival. Una saw the look on his face and put him straight.

'Look, Ice. I don't want him dead. None of us girls want him dead. He was fun, but his fun gets a bit one-sided. That's all. We just want to teach him a small lesson.' She indicated how small with her finger and thumb.

'You're not going to cut . . .'

Una laughed. 'Cut off his cock? Heaven forbid. There's plenty of pleasure for that to give yet. Oh no. That's not what I've got in mind.'

She settled back into her seat again.

'Drive me to Kitty's, will you?'

She didn't really expect an answer, so he didn't give one.

They drove in silence, her mind full of plans for the future, his full of fear.

Once she got to Kitty's, she got out and told Ice to wait for her.

He watched her walk away, her feet bare, the harsh denim of the huge overalls hanging like a sack around her slim figure.

When she came back out, Kitty was with her. Una wore a dress that shimmered and sparkled with layer after layer of dark blue crystals. Because Kitty was a little larger than her, the neckline gaped so that her breasts were barely covered.

'You're not wearing any underwear,' he remarked as she leaned on the side of the car. He could see right down the gaping neckline to the dark posy beyond her stomach.

Una laughed.

'Take us to Gloria's,' she ordered next.

He slipped the car into gear and drove off. The girls were laughing and chattering in the back. He liked the sound of their voices and the way their stockings made a rasping sound as they crossed one silky leg over the other. If he looked in the mirror at the just the right angle, he could see the naked flesh above their stocking tops. And he wasn't imagining the dark clefts lying like a furry animal between their legs.

Chapter 17

How Una, Kitty and Gloria kept the fact secret from Blue, Ice never knew and didn't ask about.

Unlike a large number of similar establishments, Amazons, as the club came to be called, was situated on the first floor of a small, run down building that might once have been a home to a family of means.

Fat, white pillars stood on either side of the doorway. Chandeliers sparkled from windows cleaned and polished. Eight marble steps led up to the front door. Inside, furniture, curtains, and paintwork were reminiscent of the nineteenth rather than the twentieth century.

Once the main building work was out of the way, the girls took great delight in designing and arranging the general layout of furniture.

Ice eyed it speculatively and not without misgiving.

'What are you looking so worried about?' Una slipped her arms around his waist and planted a quick kiss on his lips. The brightness in her eyes made him smile. He shook his head as if he were lost.

'I'm afraid for you, but I'm also proud of you.' He kissed her back. 'Are you sure you women are after revenge? This place looks like a . . .' he paused before saying the word and looked shyly away.

'A bordello?' Una finished.

He blinked as he nodded. 'I thought you were after revenge.'

'We are! But first, we have to lure the creature into our trap, and what better way to bait a trap than to use honey. Our prey must have no fear when he enters here. He must feel that this place, like women, are designed purely for his amusement and the satisfaction of men like him. Like the velvet sofas and the sparkling chandeliers, the women here must appear decorative, not threatening.'

Ice smiled and rubbed at her arms. 'You amaze me,' he said, and frowned. 'But how have you paid for all this?'

'Not with my body,' she replied, her eyes full of amusement. 'The money was bequeathed by a patron of Gloria.'

Ice raised his eyebrows. Gloria set down a tray of coffee on the low table beside them.

'Sit down,' she said. 'I'll tell you all about it over coffee.'

Ice did as ordered, finding a two-seater settee more comfortable than a chair. Besides, Una could sit beside him.

'It was like this,' Gloria began. 'I was sixteen and orphaned, so I had to go and live with my uncle and aunt on New York's East Side. My aunt was my father's sister. Although she was strict, she was quite happy to have me. My uncle wasn't quite so keen. He agreed to the idea as long as I went out to work. He wasn't keeping no slip of a girl in food and stockings, he said. Accordingly, I went to work in a general store where you could buy anything from a tin pot to a sack of flour. It was OK – for a while.'

'Anyway, Bowen, who ran the place, had a roving eye, and although I led him on a bit, I didn't fancy him. He got annoyed about that, said he would report me to my uncle if I wasn't nice to him. But I was stubborn and, besides, I enjoyed egging him on, seeing his eyes bulging out of his head, and his tongue licking his dribbling lips. It was naughty of me, but it became like a drug. After egging him on, I was pretty uptight myself, so I used to sneak into the store room and do delicious things with my body until I was back to normal.'

Kitty shot her a disbelieving look.

'Well,' Gloria sniggered. 'Almost normal. Anyway, one day he caught me at it, said I was a naughty girl and he would tell my uncle.

'"Bend over those sacks," he said. I had no choice. I had to do it. So I bent over the sacks. He lifted my skirt and pulled my knickers down. Then he spanked me until I was crying, then once I was crying, he turned me over and said he'd give me something to make me feel better. So that was it. He had his wicked way.

'It would have gone on like that, if it hadn't been for Conan McCorkindale.'

'Do you mean *the* Conan McCorkindale?' Kitty asked with raised eyebrows

Gloria nodded. 'One and the same. Bowen and him had grown up together. Well, one day he came waltzing in without us hearing him. Bowen had found fault with me about something and was making my bottom pink and warm – just as he liked it. Just as he was about to unbutton himself, Conan made himself known. Bowen was dumbstruck.

'"Bowen," said Conan, "I'm ashamed of you." He put his arm around me and held me close. He smelt of cologne and Harris Tweed. Not like Bowen. He smelt of beef fat and stale tobacco.'

'"This girl is wasted here," he said and smiled the biggest and best smile I've ever seen. "How about working for me?" he said. "Mind, it will mean living in my house rather than with your parents."

'I explained I had no parents. "Then that's settled," he said.

So that was how I met my benefactor, Conan McCorkindale.'

'And that,' said Kitty looking wryly at Ice, 'is how we've got the money to do this place. Conan might be married and have six children, but I think his wife is strictly missionary position. No hanky spanky for her!'

They laughed, and Ice smiled. He looked up into Una's eyes as she touched his arm.

'Don't worry,' she said softly. 'We'll be alright. It's all planned, except for the final showdown, and we need you to help us with that. You will help us, won't you?'

He saw the concern in her eyes. How could he let her down?

He nodded. 'Of course I'll help you.'

That night as she lay in his arms with her belly pressed against his, he wondered exactly what he was letting himself in for. He also wondered at Blue's punishment and decided whose shoes he preferred to be in.

'Hell hath no fury,' he whispered.

'What was that you said?' Una asked.

'Nothing. I was just thinking how easy it is for love to turn to hate.'

He smothered any further questions with hot kisses, his tongue demanded entry into her mouth, and his member rose from its nest of hair to nudge between her pubic lips.

Chapter 18

Father Sean O'Flanagan smiled as Rosa and a skipping Maria walked towards him. His eyes slid naturally from mother to daughter. He started at the colour of Maria's eyes. Where her mother's were brown, hers were as blue and bright as his own. It was almost, he thought, like looking in the mirror and seeing a younger and more feminine version of himself looking out.

Rosa stopped, smiled and he thought he saw the slight blush of guilt colour her cheeks. To think she might be thinking of times past fired his senses in a way no priest was supposed to be fired.

'Good day, Rosa. Maria.' He was sure his voice gave away no trace of what he was feeling inside. It wasn't guilt. It was a gnawing awareness that his hunger for another man's wife would never go away.

'Father O'Flanagan. I wanted to ask you if you had chance to speak to my eldest son.'

Sean nodded. 'I did.'

His smile was thin, and a slight trace of a frown wrinkled his brow.

Rosa sighed. 'So he didn't listen.'

Sean shook his head. 'Your son does not appear to have any plans for matrimony. He has cut his life out in the shape he wants it. I have done all I can.'

He saw the troubled look in her eyes; wanted to reach out for her, hold her close and pat her glorious hair as her head lay on his shoulder.

But he couldn't do that. He was her priest despite having been her lover.

Rosa sighed. He remembered her sighing like that after having made love to her. A wave of satisfaction had covered them both like the softest, the most delicate of silk sheets, caressing their bodies with the same coolness that lifts a butterfly's wings or drifts across a lake like mist in the early morning.

'It hurts to think that my son will not tell his own mother where he is or what he is doing. It hurts even more to learn from a stranger that he has no intention of settling down.'

Sean winced. A stranger. Was that truly what he was?

Rosa saw his expression. Her fingers touched his arm before she realised what she was doing. 'I'm sorry.' She withdrew her hand as though the sleeve of his dark serge jacket had burned her fingertips. 'I didn't mean to imply that you are a stranger like some people are strangers. I mean, that you are someone outside the family.'

As she looked into his eyes, he glanced meaningfully at Maria. Rosa looked away.

'But you did your best,' she said. 'I can expect nothing more.'

'When I see him again, I will stress the point. After all, if he does not intend to marry, he might just as well be a priest.'

Recognising the ridiculousness of such a statement, they both burst into laughter. It was Maria who brought them back down to earth.

'Blue likes watching naked women. He likes having lots of wives. He told me so.'

Shocked, both adults looked at the beaming Maria.

'Child!' Rosa shook her. 'Tell me the truth, you little minx.'

'Rosa!' Sean lay his hand on her arm as her actions became more vigorous.

'I heard them!' cried Maria on the verge of tears. 'I heard him and Tony. They said they were going to a new club where only women work and their uniform is exactly the same as Eve's was in the garden of Eden. I knew what they meant. I know that Eve didn't wear any clothes. At least, not at first. Not until she met the serpent.'

Sean straightened. His face was flushed and he found it difficult now to look into Rosa's face. Had not he himself been beguiled by the serpent? And Eve?

He looked more objectively at the beautiful Maria who was obviously sullied by a vivid imagination and a proclivity to lie. Everything in Eden, he realised, was not perfect.

Never would he regret having lain with and loved his beautiful Rosa. But that didn't mean to say that some form of penance was not due.

'Where is this nightclub that Blue and Tony spoke of?' he asked Maria.

'Amazons,' she said.

After wishing Rosa and her daughter – their daughter – good day, Sean turned away and retreated into the cool darkness of the nave. Before the altar, he tried to pray, but although he looked suitably pious, his heart ached and there was a pounding in his head.

Had the devil come to tempt him? In his heart of hearts he knew that no devil was responsible for the fire in his loins. Memories of Rosa stalked his waking hours as well as his sleeping ones. Although the crucifix shone silver and bright above the altar, in his mind he saw only the naked body of the woman he loved, writhing in expectation as he leaned above her.

He had fallen for her charms. The powerful attraction between them had bound them together as tightly as chains. Or very strong elastic. They might spring apart, but could not let go of each other.

Perhaps, he thought, if I save Blue from himself I might save myself also.

In the obstinate starkness of his bedroom, he stripped off his clothes and washed himself with cold water. He needed to be alert. He also needed to cool the heat of his flesh. There were many confessions between now and the time the nightclubs and speakeasies sprang into decadent life. Once the church was quiet and the night was dark, he would sneak away into the wild side of life and see what he could do to assuage his own guilt.

Rosa Bonecci had an appointment with the doctor after leaving the priest.

Maria was left out in the waiting room with only the receptionist for company. Rosa always went along to see Doctor Cohen at the end of his surgery. She hated waiting, she said, preferring everyone else to go in first.

After the doctor had carefully locked the door behind her, Rosa began to disrobe.

'Just your knickers will do,' said the doctor. 'And undo your blouse so that I can examine your chest.'

Rosa did just that.

She obeyed his next demand before he had a chance to complete it. 'Lie down on the couch.'

After removing her shoes, he pulled two metal devices from the sides of the couch on which two leather straps were suspended. He placed each of her feet in these, the leather tightening around her ankles.

Carefully, he pulled her dress up and layered it over her belly. The whole of her lower torso was exposed to his view. Her sex was open and shiny pink.

As he cleared his throat, Doctor Cohen hitched his stethoscope around his neck and opened her unbuttoned dress.

'Breath in,' he said and proceeded to listen to her heartbeat. As he did this, his hand was inside her dress, his palm warm on her breast, his fingers exploring her nipple in a manner that had nothing to do with determining her health.

'Breath out,' he ordered. His hand examined her other breast. She gave little cries of delight as each one was thoroughly felt, pummelled and tweaked.

'They are wonderful!' he exclaimed. 'Now let us see if you have any problems anywhere else.'

His hand now rested on her sex. He pulled the lips of her sex apart with the fingers of one hand. With the other, he placed the round head of the stethoscope onto her clitoris.

She bit her lip and closed her eyes.

'How does that feel?' he asked.

'It makes me tremble,' she replied.

'And this?'

She gave a little cry as his finger slid into her vagina, but made no comment. Her eyes closed, and she bit her bottom lip.

Lying thus, she felt waves of pleasure burst over her just as she had in her youth. Tinker, tailor, soldier, sailor. In her youth it had not mattered what profession a man had. All he needed was the right touch and his key was in the door.

It had been over ten years ago when her sexual appetite had become jaded and she had sought the most taboo places, the most respected of men to give her the satisfaction she craved.

Maria, of course, had been something of a mistake. But her husband had accepted her as his own. Nevertheless, a thrill still ran through her when she saw the look in Father Sean O'Flanagan's eyes each time she paraded Maria before him.

Guilt had taken hold of the Catholic priest's heart and pulled him from her arms. A variety of different men had since taken his place. The good doctor who now unleashed his weapon and pushed it into her with all the cold precision of his chosen profession, was the latest in a long line of lovers.

He never lay full stretch on her: never kissed her. He merely stood between her bent knees, his hands beneath her bottom as he thrust into her.

'Does this feel better?' he asked.

'Yes, doctor!'

Sometimes she eyed him through narrowed eyes: his dark brows, his bespectacled eyes just inches from the stirrups that held her ankles.

It was best to close her eyes, to drift off into that fantastic somewhere where she was young again and men were dark-haired, fiery-eyed and blessed with a virility and an imagination to set her pulse racing.

As she did so, all the old sensations became bright again, became new. Like the wings of butterflies, they started where his body slammed against hers and made her flesh drip with nectar. Then the trembling, gentle, warm feelings spread out like so many lace fingers.

The good doctor increased his pace. Her own responses kept time with him. Slowly, quicker, more slowly again, spreading upwards, outwards, and deep into her very soul.

'An injection!' the doctor shouted. 'You must have an injection!'

She cried out: a long, soulful 'Ooooow' of satisfaction as his fluid pumped into her.

Maria was sitting on the corner of the receptionist's desk when Rosa closed the door of the doctor's consulting room behind her.

The receptionist, a red-haired woman with a large bust and an even larger behind, looked up, her smile friendly, her eyes squinting behind the thick glasses she wore.

'Feeling better, Mrs Bonecci?' she asked.

'Oh, yes,' Rosa replied with subdued enthusiasm. 'I always feel much better after the doctor gives me an injection.' She turned to Maria. 'I hope you have been a good girl.'

'She's been very good,' the receptionist interjected, and Maria beamed.

By the time Rosa had reached the bottom of the stairs that led from the doctor's consulting rooms to the street, her mind had already turned back to her son and her worries about his wayward attitude to women.

If anyone had known her own sexual habits, few would have understood her attitude to those of her son. But Rosa was basically a loyal and loving wife. A marriage, she believed, was a good base for living and loving. It gave a meaning to existence. Everything else, including sex without commitment, was merely a pleasure.

Chapter 19

They enjoyed buying the things they needed to furnish the club. They even enjoyed supervising the workmen and placing furniture and decorative bits of china around.

But it was hard work, and much as they enjoyed it, there were times when they just collapsed on the comfortable furniture and talked about Blue and the things they had done with him.

'That bastard had me out without any underwear on one day,' Kitty remarked. 'It was a cold day too. I could have caught my death!'

Gloria gulped her tea down before she could get out exactly what she wanted to say. 'He made me sit with my tits out as we drove along the road. I got frightened. I thought a cop might arrest me and I started to put them away. He wouldn't let me. He grabbed hold of my tit and pulled me to him. He kissed me and told me he liked me to be exciting. I'd never heard it called that before. I thought it was brazen. Kind of cheap.'

Kitty and Una exchanged glances. The contradictions in what she was saying were obviously lost on Gloria.

For the most part, Una kept her own counsel on what

she and Blue had done together. How could she have believed she had loved him and he had loved her? It all seemed so stupid now, so why wouldn't she tell tales about him?

But that was her nature. Every lover she had ever had was special to her. Right from the very start, she had regarded her body and that of her lover with respect. Blue was no exception. Thinking that way went right back to Raven. Raven was only part of his name. He was called Raven that Flies in the Night. Unlike her, he was full Cherokee. She was only half.

They had grown up together. They had hunted the same woods, fished in the same streams and swam naked in the same lakes.

As they had got older, they still swam naked together. Like Eden, she thought. That was how her wilderness had been before Blue Bonecci had come along. She did not count Ice in the same breath. He was different, though she had not really known that at the time.

It had been a hot summer day when she and Raven had run breathlessly to the lake, disrobed and threw themselves into the cool, sparkling water.

They had swum strongly, diving beneath the surface like the beaver, clambering up the waterfalls to follow the leaping sock-eye salmon.

When at last they had grown tired from their efforts, they had sought the shade of the trees which trailed their branches in the lake.

Breathless, they had thrown themselves down in the cool long grass and gazed spellbound at the dancing sunlight that filtered through the leaves above their heads.

She had closed her eyes then, vaguely aware that someone had touched her, she opened them again.

Raven had been staring down at her, gazing at her breasts, her belly and the pubic hair that was growing between her legs.

Silently, she had looked into his eyes. She had opened her mouth to say something. He had raised a finger before his lips. 'Be quiet.'

She had remained silent, then watched as he wove a bunch of grasses together, then pressed them between his hands. She had thought he was in prayer. He had closed his eyes and began singing a low, humming sound that hardly seemed to have any words at first.

Her body had trembled as she'd watched him. Not because she was afraid of what he might do, but because something had happened between them.

She could not see any difference between them, except that hairs now grew around their sexual parts, and her breasts had become round and firm like ripe, young apples.

She eyed his body for other signs of change. Her gaze went automatically to the thick bush of black hair that sprouted between his legs. For the first time ever, she noticed that his penis was not the gentle, soft thing that reminded her of a tree root mushroom, but was bigger, stiffer, its end glistening with a droplet of what looked like dew.

That was the physical sign, along with her own bodily alterations.

But there was still that something she could not see, an intangible thing that was there between them, drawing one body to the other, gripping the heart with an intense feeling of affection and a need to touch, to cling, to fuse together as one.

Youthful flesh tingling, she watched through narrowed eyes, her breath catching in her throat as he began to brush her flesh with the bunch of wild grasses. The effect was not unpleasant.

Up and down her body went the bunch of grass. He never stopped chanting as he did it.

The heads of the grasses tickled her flesh and made the sensations she was feeling increase and spread like wildfire all over her body.

Palpitations seemed to echo around her rib cage. There was a heaviness between her legs that she had not noticed before. She also sensed that there was a wetness there that did not come from the grass she lay on, but from her own body.

So great was the turmoil inside her, that she pleaded with her eyes that Raven should end her torment. He had told her to be quiet, so she kept pleading with her eyes, although she did not know exactly what he could do to save her.

It was no good. She had to say something.

'Do something,' she said simply.

He shrugged, and she wondered when his muscles had become so much more pronounced. Was it at the same time as his penis had grown? She had not noticed it before.

Suddenly, his face seemed to harden with concentration.

'I don't know what to do,' he said, then corrected himself. 'I mean, I do, but . . .' he paused. 'I'm not too sure. I don't want to hurt you.'

'You could never hurt me,' she said softly, and reached for his hand.

He let the bunch of grass drop. She laid his hand on her young breast and for the first time, felt the fire of true sexuality rush through her body.

There had been nothing but gentleness in that first time with Raven. There had been many other couplings between them, but nothing could match that very first time when each had explored the other's body, and each had experienced urges bestowed by nature, but exploited by humankind.

After yet another lot of effort put into getting the club ready for opening, Kitty suggested they take a break.

'How about a movie?'

Douglas Fairbanks was playing in something that was swashbuckling, but full of romance. The movie house was fairly local, so the three of them took a trolley rather than a car or a taxi.

Kitty dozed once or twice during the film, but Una and Gloria watched it till the end.

By the time it had finished, and by the time they had debated over how they should get home, the streets were emptying and the sidewalks beginning to glisten with rain.

'Looks like we'll be walking,' sulked Gloria. 'In these shoes!'

She pointed to the open-toed shoes she was wearing. The toes of her stockings were already wet.

All three of them looked up as a car drew gently into the kerb.

'Kitty? Kitty Malone?'

Dazzling blue eyes looked up from under a soft brown trilby. Kitty stepped forward.

'Johnnie Angel! Well, how are you?'

'Fine,' he replied his eyes raking her up and down. 'But I'm sure not so fine as you.'

Kitty suddenly seemed to sparkle from head to toe. Una nudged Gloria and exchanged a questioning look.

They took a step back as the man got out of his car. He was tall, and once his hat was removed, a crop of corn-coloured hair toppled over his forehead. His smile seemed permanent.

Kitty took hold of his arm. 'Girls. This is Johnnie Angel. An old friend.'

'How do you do?'

They exchanged polite nods.

Una briefly wondered what mob he belonged to. Then she saw the shoulder holster; the neat cut of his suit, the straightness of his tie. J. Edgar Hoover liked his boys to be well turned out. Tidiness was like a uniform with him. That's why it was so easy to recognise a G-man.

'You one of Blue's boys?' an unwitting Gloria asked.

Kitty looked bashful. Johnnie Angel's beaming smile got even wider.

It was Una who straightened things out.

'No, Gloria. He's one of J. Edgar Hoover's mob. He's a Fed.'

'Oh!' Gloria's mouth dropped open.

Johnnie's arm snaked around Kitty's back.

'Look, honey. I'm killing some time at the moment. Are you free, or are you and your friends off somewhere special?'

Kitty looked awkwardly at the other two. Gloria looked shell-shocked. Una looked thoughtful. Something resembling revelation came to her eyes.

'We're going back to our place of business,' she said quickly and smiled almost as widely as he did. 'You can come with us if you like.'

Kitty and Gloria looked astonished. Una and Johnnie hardly seemed to notice their unease.

'What sort of business?' Johnnie asked.

'A nightclub,' replied an unabashed Una. 'A very special nightclub run by women for women.' She flashed a quick look in Kitty's direction. 'I'm sure Kitty would agree with me that we'd like to keep on the right side of the law so, perhaps you'd like to take a look at it.'

She struck a provocative pose, hands on hips, stockinged leg swivelling from side to side.

Johnnie's white teeth kept showing through his smile. He tilted his hat back away from his eyes. In that moment, Una knew what his answer would be, though Kitty looked terrified.

'What could be better than spending some time with beautiful, law-abiding dames like you? Of course I'll cast my eye over things. Anything to help.'

On the drive over to Amazons in Johnnie Angel's sleek, Government issue car, the girls' nervousness turned to giggles of excitement.

'Can I feel your holster?' Una asked, her arm draped over Johnnie's shoulder.

'Feel what you want. Be my guest.'

Gloria giggled. 'Oooow, yes please.'

Una exchanged a quick look with Kitty who was sitting next to Johnnie.

By the time they got to the club, a party atmosphere had taken hold of the female occupants of the car, and the driver didn't look too unhappy either.

Kitty had taken a lead from Una and was sliding her hand from the handle of Johnnie's colt, down over the tan leather holster, over his waist and onto his crotch.

Gloria was draped around his neck, her bright red lips leaving smudged imprints all over his cheek, round his neck, and even onto the pure whiteness of his shirt collar.

Smiling triumphantly, Una sat back in the seat, her eyes bright. Like the pieces of a jigsaw, everything was beginning to slide firmly into place. Johnnie was a bonus. What better licence than a Government one? Blue couldn't possibly stop them from opening, and doubtless wouldn't. She promised herself that she'd tell Ice as quickly as possible.

'This joint is yours?' Johnnie asked incredulously as all three looked in on the main room where the central chandelier was picked out by the streetlight that shone just outside the window.

'Doesn't it leave you breathless?' Kitty said to him.

He lowered his face close to her ear. 'Not as breathless as you used to leave me.'

They huddled close. Gloria reached for the light switch.

'No!' It was Una who stayed her hand. 'Leave it off,' she murmured. 'The room looks just as good with the light off.' She stepped outside the door leaving the three of them within its shadows. 'I'll get us some drinks. Take care of our friend from the FBI.'

Gloria caught her wink and glanced from her to Kitty and her friend, Johnnie, who was already reacting to Kitty's erotic body language.

'Is this arm going free?' She looped her arm through his.

When Una last looked, the Federal Agent was being eased towards the large, red velvet settee that had room for five people, and possibly more.

When she was sure their attention was elsewhere, Una stepped smartly to the telephone that hung in a curtained kiosk just inside the front door. She dialled a number.

'Ice?'

Someone on the other end asked who wanted him.

'Amelia,' she replied. Amelia was the code word they used whenever they thought Blue might be present. It was his mother's name.

The gruff voice on the other end went off to find him.

'Amelia. Nice to hear your voice.' He sounded puzzled.

'Ice. I've got someone here who might be useful to us.'

'Like who?'

'A Federal Agent named Johnnie Angel.'

There was silence from the other end of the phone. Had he gone? Had outrageous misfortune intervened and an adversary overheard and drawn his own conclusion?

'Ice? Are you still there?'

'Yes. I'm still here. I was just thinking.'

'He could be useful. Are you coming over?'

'How useful were you hoping he'd be?'

Una got closer to the wall, her back facing the room where Gloria and Kitty were already doing their work. Every so often there came a cry of pleasure, a low moan of wishes fulfilled.

'I think our government friend is easily compromised. Do you wish to confront him, or shall I?'

His answer was immediate. 'I'll be right over.'

The building was still in semi-darkness when he arrived. Una watched him get out of his car then come swiftly and silently up the steps to the front door. She already had it ajar.

'Come in,' she whispered.

His lips fastened on hers as she let him through the narrow gap and closed the door behind him.

Perhaps it was the excitement running through her like a sharp shock of electricity. Or perhaps it was the very fact that it was dark and sounds of love-making came tumbling out of the door behind them.

'He sounds as if he's enjoying himself,' Ice whispered, his breath mingling with hers, his lips still hovering over her face.

Understanding flashed between them.

'Let's go look see,' Una whispered.

Like silent spectres, they glided to the open door. Una stood transfixed. Ice stood behind her, his body close to hers. His hand came to rest on her hip. She felt it tense as he took in the scene before them. For a moment, she too held her breath.

The Federal Agent was laid full stretch on the floor. His clothes were scattered over the plush, red settee along with the more lightweight attire of Gloria and Kitty.

Naked and glistening in the light that filtered through the window, Gloria sat astride his head. She heard sucking sounds similar to that of a cat or a dog lapping up a saucer of milk. But Johnnie Angel was not lapping up milk. He was lapping at nectar, the honeyed juice of Gloria's sexual arousal.

Una felt her lover's hand run up from her hip to rest just below her breast. She wondered whether he could feel her heart beating.

Kitty was astride the man's pelvis. Although it wasn't possible to see for sure whether she had mounted his prick, Una was pretty certain she had. Her head was thrown back, her throat white in what light there was, and she was moaning as she slammed up and down against his hips.

Every so often, Kitty would lean forward and retrieve the man's hands which were gripping Gloria's buttocks. She then placed these on her breasts, and each time, she sighed, mewed and almost screamed with pleasure.

Una became aware of Ice moving nearer, his erection hard against her buttocks. She sucked in her breath, unable to move, unable to make any noise at all. Like him, her gaze was fixed on the scene in the darkened room.

A draught of air she had not noticed before brushed the tops of her thighs. Had she left a door open? Suddenly, she realised what it was. Her skirt was being rolled slowly up over her thighs, her hips. A warm hand and probing fingers slid between her legs and undid the buttons of her French knickers.

Her jaw dropped. Her wet tongue ran excitedly over her dry lips as his hand ran between her legs. Sexual juices seeped freely along her slit and over his fingers. There was a slurping sound as his fingers explored her vagina, testing the warmth, the liquidity of her hidden portal.

She opened her mouth wider to gasp, but no sound came out. It was as though she was suspended in animation; frozen with passion, and bound by the fibrous ropes of unquenchable desire.

His fingers left her, though she could still feel his knuckles working, undoing something behind her. Buttons, she thought. Her guess was confirmed as the hot, wet head of his penis poked into the gully that separated her golden orbs. What had been merely a cleft between was widened. This snake, this tool that prodded her, was widening her channel to suit itself. It was dipping into her vagina, stealing a crown of slippery wetness, then transferring that wetness onto the bunched opening between her buttocks.

Oblivious to their presence, the tableau before them continued.

Gloria's ample breasts trembled and swayed as she rode the agent's mouth. She spread her fingers over them, her nipples peeping out from the gap between.

Hips jerking up and down for all she was worth, Kitty leaned forward on her hands, her breasts swinging backwards and forwards over Johnnie Angel's outspread palms.

The whole atmosphere of the room seemed to have become satiated with sex, throbbing with uncontrollable urges that have been in existence since time immemorial.

There seemed no division between the heavy breathing of those on the floor, and those at the door.

Their climaxes had adopted a common tempo as if each

was leading the other out into the real world.

Una now watched them through narrowed eyes. Her mouth still hung open. Her breathing was heavy.

Sensations of pleasure ran like a thousand tiny needles over her divided buttocks as her lover's member pushed into her, filling her with his seed, pulsing with the promise that this was only one occasion; that there would be others. Many others.

A terrible tingle remained in her loins. She passed her hand over her belly meaning to run it over her sexual lips and relieve the ache she was feeling. But Ice's hand got there first. His fingers found the right button at just the right time.

She threw her head back as her climax was released. Before those in the room had reached theirs, her navy silk skirt covered her again, and her lover's stiffness had softened. His penis lay sleeping in his pants.

They let those in the room reach their climax too before Ice turned the light on.

Johnnie Angel sat on the red settee wearing only his trousers and his vest. A mass of dark chest hair curled over the top of the white cotton. A twist of cigarette smoke curled up over his bent head as he considered the position his own lust had put him in. The cigarette was in his right hand. He had a coffee cup in his left, and both elbows rested on his knees.

'We're offering you a good deal here,' Ice was saying. He stood by the window, eyes swiftly scanning the street outside. 'We're offering you Blue Bonecci, but on our terms. In our way.'

'You're offering evidence of him dealing up along the

Canadian border but only after we arrest him, let him go, then re-arrest him again.' He shook his head. 'I don't understand.'

Una, who was sitting in the chair opposite him, leaned forward, her hands clasped before her, knuckles white with tension.

'Look,' she said, her eyes boring into him. 'Blue has strict habits about clubs. He takes his time about going into them. We don't have that much time. The only time he tries a new joint is when he gets hassled at the one he's presently visiting. We had fully expected to wait three months, one if we were lucky – very lucky. But if you pull this for us, he'll be so pleased to be out and about, and so hostile to where you picked him up, he'll be hot footing it here. Do you understand that?'

Johnnie Angel, still looking a little sheepish, lifted his head and looked at her. There was puzzlement in his eyes, but also admiration for the intelligent looking young woman staring back at him.

He shook his head, and for a moment Una's heart seemed to stop beating.

'Lady, or rather, ladies. I don't know what your game is, but if you nail Blue Bonecci for me, I'll play to your rules.'

Johnnie Angel looked at each of them in turn. 'OK?'

The three girls looked at each other, then at Ice. They nodded. 'OK.'

Chapter 20

Blue Bonecci, dressed in a dark blue tuxedo, white shirt, red tie and sporting a cashmere over his shoulders, laughed as he got out of his car outside the Turned Turtle Club, a speakeasy he did business with. At present, it was his favourite haunt, though he had it in mind to try the Amazon Club once it opened and he got round to it. But for now, he felt comfortable frequenting the Turned Turtle.

Garfield, his current driver, slapped him on the back and laughed with him as they made their way to the dark green door behind which the booze was good and the girls were bad.

Before making his entrance into the main part of the club, they made their way through an inner door into the more stylish part of the building where a vast oak staircase led to the upper levels and the place where he and his colleagues usually did business. Garfield, a vast man with a head that seemed to come straight out of his shoulders, stayed downstairs where he could play chess with the big guy who guarded the door.

'Greetings,' Blue cried as he entered the panelled library where Tony, his brother, Verecchia, an associate, and The

171

Prof, his bookkeeper, awaited him.

His eyes rested on Ice and his smile waned somewhat.

'I wasn't expecting you to be here.'

Suspicion played in his eyes.

'I had nowhere else to go.'

Ice sounded and looked uncompromising. Although in essence he was inferior in rank to Blue, there was no fear in his eyes and, what alarmed Blue, there was also no respect. There never had been now Blue came to think of it.

Blue nodded slowly, then took out a large cigar, clipped its end. Tony gave him a light. He began to smoke it slowly before his lips curled in a threatening sneer.

'You do now. Get out of here!'

Blue held the gaze of the taller man with the steel-grey eyes. This was one of those moments when he had to show who was top dog, who was the boss. The tension between them was almost electric.

Ice looked away and moved swiftly, his long legs gaining the door in less strides than most men. Blue watched him go.

Outside, Ice paused, his hand on the handle. He strained his ears, but heard little. Taking a deep breath, he made a right that would take him away from the main staircase and down a small winding one to the cellar below the building and the small door that led out below street level.

The staircase was dark and smelt of things long dead. At the bottom, the door was secured with a bolt at least twelve inches long.

Ice manhandled it open. Before he had time to open it fully, the man who had watched from the street earlier was in with him. He was closely followed by another six all armed with machine guns and expressions reminiscent of gargoyles on the parapets of ancient cathedrals.

'Up the stairs. Turn left. First right.'

The men hurried away.

Ice leaned against the wall as the sound of men's feet pounded the floor above him. A light shade and bulb hanging on a thin wire cord swung above his head. There was the sound of a door opening, a sudden burst of gunfire.

Who bought it? Ice wondered, and felt a sudden pang of guilt. He sincerely hoped no one was dead.

The sound of shouting lasted longer. Then there was silence swiftly followed by the thud, thud, thud of men's feet marching swiftly down the grand staircase that would take Blue and his boys out of the front door and into the street. Blue Bonecci was in the custody of the FBI.

Ice tilted the trilby he wore back on his head and leaned against the wall. He closed his eyes, glad of the coolness of stone behind him, and glad that, behind his closed lids, he saw only Una, the reason he had betrayed his one time friend.

Una.

Her voice sung in his head, rung in his ears. Suddenly, he had a great urge to see her, to tear her clothes from her body and have her savagely, quickly, and selfishly.

With long strides, he was out of the door.

Night air cooled the sweat on his face. He left his car and took no taxi. The night felt good and he welcomed the darkness. He did not want to see anyone else out and about. He did not want anyone else to see him.

His footsteps echoed around the empty streets. Una had moved from the grim room she had moved into after falling out of love with Blue. Both she and Kitty now had apartments in the same building. Gloria had one in the building next door.

In the heat of love and passion, she had given him a key. He let himself in, and without turning the light on, tore his clothes off even before he gained the bedroom.

The bedroom door was open. Soft, creamy satin covered the bed. The pillows were also of satin.

The net curtains billowed in on the night breeze. By the last rays of moonshine, he could see her head on the pillow, her hair a bluish-black against the creamy shine of satin.

On the other pillow he saw blonde hair. At first he caught his breath and felt a huge surge of anger. She had been unfaithful to him, she who had promised not to sleep with any other man. This one had his arm around her and was vaguely familiar.

In a sudden rush of recognition, he knew it was no man lying there, but Gloria. Both girls were asleep and doubtless naked. But to Ice, it didn't really matter if two girls had been playing at being lovers. Una had not betrayed him.

Spellbound and clad only in his trousers now, he stared at the two beautiful women, their creamy arms thrown across each other.

Suddenly, he was smitten with the enchantment of the scene. His heart became full of love, his body full of desire.

There could be no course of action open to him except the one he had in mind. Imagine, he thought. Man's greatest desire, to be in bed between two women. The thought made him shiver. He asked himself whether they were likely to protest. A memory of two men, one girl and a cosy cabin set high in the wilderness came back to him.

'No,' he said softly. 'Not at all.'

Silently, he stepped out of his trousers and what remained of his clothes.

Penis hard again, he stepped forward and got onto the bed.

He crawled up in between them. They murmured something as he contrived to edge between them and snuggled down under their entwined limbs.

As he did so, he sighed loud and long and closed his eyes. If it was good to go to sleep with a woman's body up against his, it was even better when it was two women in the bed.

'What?' Una said it slowly, blearily, and opened her eyes. 'Ice!'

He smiled at her. Her body came closer, pressed against his. Her arms were around him, her lips were on his, on his neck, on his chest.

Gloria stirred behind him, and her strong perfume drifted over his shoulder. He felt the thick bush of her pubic hair against his buttocks, felt her lips on his shoulders.

'Honey,' he heard her say in a sleepy voice.

Gloria did not usually do anything for his libido, but this was an exceptional circumstance. He murmured with pleasure as the warmth of their bodies pressed more positively against his. By his presence alone, he had ignited some unseen fire in them. Their torsos undulated against him like waves against a beach.

'Keep doing that,' he murmured. 'Keep doing that forever.'

Their hands seemed to be all over him at once. He felt he was drifting away on a tide of sheer decadence. Pleasure had become like a magic carpet ride, or a cloud floating in a pale blue sky.

One female hand cupped his balls, whilst another pulled on his stem. Their other hands caressed his chest, his belly, and their lips landed like butterflies on his mouth, his neck, and his chest.

He did not need to close his eyes, but when he did, the vision of what Kitty and Gloria had done to the G-man came into his head. He could still see him there, lying full stretch on the floor, one pussy in his mouth, another fixed around his cock.

The vision was a powerful one. It made his member dance in the hand that held it; made his balls quiver.

They were pulling on him, urging his sperm to come out of him, to splash over their hands. He was at no pains to stop them. His throat was dry, his voice trapped in his throat.

He was still lying on his side when Gloria's free hand began to caress his behind. As she did this, Una raised her leg, bent her knee and rested it over his leg. Her pussy came closer. Her sexual lips opened, and her mouth clamped swiftly over his.

Springing like a creature from cover, his prick leapt forward, its head nudging into the fleshy crack between her thighs.

It was so easy, so delicious to slide into her. With a thrust of his pelvis, half his weapon gained entry. With a second thrust, his whole length filled her body. His pubic hair rasped against hers.

All the while, Gloria's hand caressed his behind and crept into the gap between his legs to play with his balls.

The sensations from this were incredible. Gloria was manipulating his balls, not just for his benefit or her own, but also for that of Una. As Gloria's caresses became more positive, his whole body seemed to surge into Una, his penis swelling under pressure from what was happening within and without.

Every vein in his neck felt as if were bursting. Every fibre of his being was helpless in their hands.

Just when he felt he had reached the zenith of their ministrations, Gloria's finger ran down between his cheeks and jabbed fiercely at the aperture between. He cried out, his back arching, his pelvis thudding against that of Una.

It was as if he had been speared; as if he was no more than a monkey on a stick dancing to someone else's tune.

His essence spurted out of him. Even if he had wanted to hold it back, to play for time until Una had reached her orgasm, he could not have done so.

Whatever these women wanted, they would take. And whatever they wanted, he would give it to them.

Una kissed him once he was fully spent. Her fingers ran through his hair, slid down over his ear. She traced circles around its outer edge.

He looked into her eyes. Even in the semi-darkness of the room, they still sparkled. Again, he felt helpless.

'We haven't finished with you yet,' she whispered.

Gloria giggled behind him. Suddenly he became aware that her finger was still embedded in his anus. He tried to wriggle off.

'Not so fast,' Gloria said against his ear. 'Didn't you hear what Una said? We haven't finished with you yet.'

'Greedy girls,' he said. 'What do you want now?'

Their bodies became like clothes that fitted a little too tightly.

'We're going to give you a bit of what Blue's going to get, but not quite so much. Just a little taste, that's all.'

They stretched his arms over his head and tied his wrists to the towering posts of the cast iron bed.

A sudden worry crossed his mind.

'Is this going to hurt?'

'Not much.' It was Gloria who answered.

He began to struggle.

Una lay her hands on his chest. Her lovely face came close to his.

'Don't worry, my darling. Lie back and enjoy it.'

Gloria got out of bed and went to the bathroom. He could hear her using the lavatory.

When she came back, she held a long, orange coloured bottle in one hand.

'What's that?' he asked as she took out the stopper.

'Oil,' murmured Una as she flicked her fingers at his hair and kissed his brow. 'Don't worry. It's only oil.'

His lips suddenly felt incredibly dry. He ran his tongue over them. They did not improve.

Gloria's fingers fastened around his limp weapon.

He groaned. 'Oh, no! Not again!'

The girls cuddled up to him.

'But darling. You've had what you came for. Now what about us?' Una exclaimed.

178

'That's right, darling,' added Gloria. 'You might think it's just fun going to bed with two women, but every pleasure has to be paid for. Two women are hard work – as you, my darling, are about to find out!'

To his own great surprise, his stiffness returned. Una and Gloria stroked his purple-veined protrusion which was already delivering a spit of salt-laden juice from its throbbing head.

Despite his fear of not being able to perform – because fear was really what it was all about – he found himself murmuring with pleasure. Their hands were all over him, stroking his chest, his belly, nibbling at his ears, his neck and his throat.

Una's mouth covered his and suppressed the groan that accompanied Gloria's nibbling of his balls. He could feel her soft cheeks against his inner thighs, her nose against his stem.

Strong and newly virile, his penis stood up. Chest heaving, he watched as Una got astride his pelvis and lowered herself onto his phallus. Slowly but surely, the whole length of it disappeared into her body.

Beyond her, he could see Gloria bent between his thighs, her bottom high in the air, her teeth still nibbling at his balls as Una rode his stem.

'Sublime!' Una cried out, and threw back her head.

He knew she had come, could feel the tightening of her muscles around his stem.

The urge to catch up with her and fill her with his semen was extremely powerful, but he was not given the chance.

'My turn!' he heard Gloria cry.

They swopped places.

Ice knew he was being used, but could do nothing to stop it – not that he wanted to.

The lips of Gloria's plump pussy slid down over his length.

He groaned with pleasure as Una's pearl white teeth began nibbling at his balls.

'Give me more,' he heard Gloria say.

But he was tired, besides which it was Una he wanted, not Gloria.

'Is he letting you down?' Una asked.

'This stud is not doing his best,' Gloria responded.

'Then I'll have to deal with it,' Una said.

Ice cried out as Una's finger pushed into his anus. She did not do it a little at a time, testing to see if it pained or pleasured him. She merely pushed it straight in so that his hips rose from the bed and his penis rammed home more fiercely into Gloria's accommodating vagina.

Because the response was so fierce, he could not stop the vessel that ran the length of his penis from filling up with fluid. Neither could he stop it from racing to the end of his shaft and spilling like foaming milk into the waiting Gloria.

He didn't ask them the exact details of what they had in mind for Blue. Somehow, he didn't want to know. He just wanted to lie there in the dark with their warm bodies pressed tightly against his and dream of them and him, not them and a bootleg runner named Blue Bonecci.

Chapter 21

Una wore a red dress that positively dripped with crystal beads. She wore nothing on her head, but her black hair gleamed and clung to her face like the petals of a flower.

She had chosen silk stockings with a red dragon motif climbing from her heel and undulating up her calves. Red satin shoes completed the outfit.

Kitty had chosen green for their special night. The shift fell in a straight line to her knees, then floated out in a handkerchief hem at each corner. Tufts of red hair attempted to escape from beneath a fitted pink satin cap that dazzled with green stones pretending to be emeralds. Like Una, she wore stockings that matched her outfit. Instead of red dragons, a profusion of green shamrock erupted from out of her shoes and bloomed on her legs.

Gloria wore virgin white, though virginity had not lasted long in her life. Her lipstick was red, her laugh loud, and if anybody wondered about her laughter, they would merely have put it down to high spirits. But Gloria was nervous and couldn't help disappearing in the direction of the powder room.

Unlike the others', her stockings were plain at the heel

but dotted with loads of sparkling sequins.

Kitty joined Una at the bar.

'Do you think he'll come?' she asked.

Una's gaze roamed over the clientele who had thronged into the Amazon Club, fascinated to find out more about a place that was owned and staffed entirely by women. 'How could he not come? This is the hottest spot in town, and for him it could get considerably hotter.'

The tinkle of glasses and of laughter permeated the atmosphere, but was drowned out by the raucous sound of Southern jazz as a three piece combo thrummed into action.

The heavy curtains were closed, and the chandelier sparkled before a huge panel that depicted naked women behaving less than respectably. The picture was edged with a gilt frame, and on closer scrutiny, it could be seen that it was not covered with glass as most pictures are. But then, it was a very big picture.

'No show yet!' chirped an over nervous Gloria.

'He'll be here,' said Una quietly.

She turned and ordered another martini from the girl behind the bar. Like the other staff, the girl was dressed in a red top and blue shorts. The top was cut very low so that when she bent over the bar to reach the bottles below it, her nipples showed above her neckline. The shorts were cut high at the back so that the cheeks of her behind peeped provocatively above the tops of her legs.

Even the three piece band was female. They, because of their bulk, were dressed more sedately, two in red, and one in blue. They looked the most respectable women in the place.

'What do you think he'll make of it?' Kitty asked, her

eyes flitting from Una to the jittery Gloria.

'The public rooms, or the room reserved specifically for him?'

In response to Gloria's nervousness, Kitty had begun rubbing her hands together. She stopped when Una said that and exchanged a covert look with her. A slow smile spread over her face.

'I think it will open his eyes.'

Una sipped at her drink as she surveyed the happy crowd. 'I think it will open a lot of people's eyes.'

Blue Bonecci sat with a look like thunder in the back of his car. The Feds had released him because of insufficient evidence, but had only done so once he had called the Prof in to state his legal entitlement.

Garfield, his driver, glanced at him via the rear view mirror before daring to speak.

'They had nothing on you, boss. They were just pushing their luck.'

His judgement did nothing to soothe Blue's anger. The shadow of death, or at least, revenge was in his eyes. His dark brows were beetled over his handsome, aquiline nose. His mouth was tightly closed, yet his jaw trembled with the gnashing of his teeth.

Garfield tried again. 'You wanna go make merry, boss?'

As though he had only just realised he was not alone, Blue glared in his direction.

'Do I what?'

Garfield looked suitably abashed, 'I only said . . .'

'Sure!' Blue's lockjaw lessened. 'Sure! I'm a free man.'

He laughed. 'Let's go make merry.'

Garfield's white teeth flashed as he smiled. 'Great, boss. Turned Turtle here we come.'

'No!' Blue's hand landed heavily on his shoulder. 'No! Not the Turned Turtle. Bad memories, Garfield. Besides...' he leaned back thoughtfully in his seat. 'There's a chance that someone there had a hand in this. There's also a chance that the Feds might be back there looking for me.'

He went quiet.

Garfield waited, slowing the car until the boss told him exactly where he was going.

Blue's hand rested in front of his mouth whilst he considered. Then he looked up. 'That new club. The one run by broads. Take me there.'

Glad to see his employer back on form, Garfield beamed. 'Sure boss. You mean the Amazon Club.' The car sped forward down Main Street, and off into the side roads where the street lights were less bright and the night life more decadent.

A sudden thought made Garfield ease off the gas.

'Boss, I don't know for sure, but I think I heard a rumour about the Amazon Club. Something about it being a bit select.'

'Are you saying they won't let me in?'

'Well ... They might not. I've just got a feeling I heard that the members are all ...'

Blue did not give him a chance to finish.

'Garfield, you get me there. Leave it to me to get in the door.'

Troubled, but knowing when to keep his mouth shut,

Garfield stepped on the gas. Eventually, they pulled up outside a place where a woman warrior with one breast, a bow and a quiverful of arrows over her shoulder, glowed in red lights above a whitewashed portico.

'Wait for me here,' Blue ordered.

Grinning confidently, he took out a huge cigar, lit it, then rearranged the cashmere coat that lay heavily on his shoulders.

'Select membership, eh? Well kiss my butt!'

The door opened almost before he had time to heave the brass knocker against it. It was a woman who answered. She was big and black, her shoulders broad. Each of her breasts was big enough to use as a pillow.

Alert to any attempt by her to bar him entry – and she was big enough to do it – he stepped quickly inside the door.

'Good evening, sir. We've been expecting you.'

'You have?' He told himself she had obviously mistaken him for someone else. Either that or she knew exactly who he was.

'May I take your coat?'

'Certainly. May I ask you something?'

'Certainly, sir. Always happy to be of service.'

She smiled broadly, the picture of servile domesticity. Yet he sensed that underneath that homespun exterior, someone with the reach and punch of a heavyweight boxer was struggling to get out.

'Do you know who I am?' He stood with legs apart as he said it, his chest thrust forward, stomach tightly tensed, and arms held away from his side. The cigar remained in his right hand.

The woman smiled benevolently. 'Sure, sir. You're Mr Bonecci, and you're expected.'

He blinked, 'I am?'

Immediately, it became apparent to him just how important he was. There again, he told himself, haven't you already been told that this place is run by a bunch of dames? How many of them, he wondered, were past acquaintances, women whose bodies he'd tasted then discarded like spent chicken bones.

He grinned and rolled his shoulders as though he were about to enter the ring.

'Fine by me,' he exclaimed, and made his way in the direction the woman indicated.

The smell of the place was as glorious as the decor. Odours of female perfumes and female bodies washed over him. He adored the decor. Wouldn't any man? Everything was plush velvet and all of it scarlet. A huge painting of sorts caught his eye. He couldn't help but admire it. It was huge and the subject was women, and the women were naked and doing all the things he loved them to do.

A young woman in blue knocked into him.

'Sorry, darling,' she said throatily, then proceeded to look him up and down in the way he assessed women.

'Had a good look?' he asked, wondering if she was worth his while getting to know better.

'For now,' she tittered, and danced away.

For once in his life, he had the strangest sensation that he was a woman, or at least a sex object being scrutinised before being seduced.

Being careful not to return the looks of the women he

passed, he made his way to the bar.

The moment he saw them there, his face broke into smiles. This, he told himself, could be a happy night. The giggling Gloria, the sophisticated Kitty, and the enigmatic Una were standing at the bar. He headed straight for them.

'Well, well, well. Looks as though they let all sorts in here.'

Each of them offered her cheek for a welcome kiss. He squeezed each of their breasts as he kissed them. He did not see the exchange of looks between them.

'You're all looking good!' He spread his arms as he said it, his face beaming with happiness and already hinting at lust.

'Do we?' piped up Gloria.

'Good as what?' Kitty added.

Una was to the point. 'As good as hunting trophies. That's how he's looking at us. See the look in his eyes? We're merely hunting trophies. Medals to be hung on a wall and dusted off now and again.'

At first his jaw fell open. Then he laughed.

'Oh, come on girls. We had our fun. But things change. People change.'

'Like us,' Una interrupted. 'We've changed.'

'Yes,' he said without his smile diminishing. 'You've all changed. You're all more beautiful than ever.'

'Bullshit!' Una turned away.

Blue got between Gloria and Kitty and ordered a drink from the bar. He glanced briefly at Una. His smile had gone and there was a troubled look in his eyes. He remembered the feel of her body and wondered whether he had made a terrible mistake in dumping her this early. Another session with her might be fun. Another six sessions wouldn't be out of the question.

He held a dollar out to the barmaid. The barmaid exchanged a glance with Una.

'It's on the house. With Miss Una,' she said, and walked away.

Blue's mouth dropped open. He shifted on the bar, and slugged his drink. His eyes stayed glued on Una.

'Am I getting the right picture here? Did she say on the house and Miss Una?'

Una nodded. The other two held themselves that bit straighter. 'You heard right.'

'This is your place?'

They all exchanged looks then looked back at him. There was no need for words. He only had to look at their faces to know they were telling the truth.

'Well, I'll be damned!'

'Drink up,' said Kitty. 'I'll get you the next one.'

'And I'll get you the one after that,' piped up Gloria.

By the time he had accepted and imbibed of their gifts, he was relaxed, but not drunk. Up until now, he had not studied the club with any great intensity, except for the huge picture of the naked women. It had surprised him to think that his discarded women now owned what looked to be a popular club.

'You've got a lot of people here,' he said, then wondered why the crowd he watched gave him such misgivings. A riot of colourful dresses danced before him, mostly women dancing with women – no. All were women dancing with women. A certain truth was gradually seeping into his brain. It was Una who prevented it seeping in too quickly.

'Would you like to look round the place?'

He tore his gaze away from the dancers and looked at her. Her eyes looked so blue, her breasts so round and firm. He tapped at her nipple with his index finger. He felt its hardness pressing against the smooth silkiness of her dress.

'Yes,' he said smiling. In his head he was seeing a room with a bed and a naked Una lying ready and waiting on it, her sex open to his view and his penis.

She led him through a door. To his surprise, Gloria and Kitty followed on behind.

Oh well, he thought. One is nice, two is heaven, and three . . . exhausting, but well worth a try.

Una placed her hand on a door knob.

'Is that the bedroom?' Blue asked.

Una paused. 'You want the bedroom?' she asked without looking round at him.

He glanced back at Kitty and Gloria. They stepped closer to him. A flutter started in his loins and quickly spread along the length of his penis.

'Yes,' he said, exchanging what he interpreted as lustful looks with Gloria and Kitty. 'I want the bedroom, and I also want both of you.'

Una turned round. The smile of her lips and her eyes reminded him of a cat he'd once hunted. Not a domestic cat, but a mountain lion with a silky tan coat and yellow eyes.

'Do you mean you want to perform for us like we used to perform for you?' she asked.

At this moment in time, her voice seduced him as much as her body.

'I do,' he replied.

Una crossed over to another door. 'Then walk into my parlour,' she said, and Blue willingly obliged.

Chapter 22

A buzz of interest ran through those gathered in the Amazon Club. Chairs were pulled into position as the screens hiding the stage were folded on their hinges. Eyes were bright with expectation, and hearts fluttered in anticipation in female breasts. Everyone had been told beforehand to be very quiet, but there was a glass screen between them and the tableau which was about to unfold.

Naked and proud, Una, Gloria and Kitty stood around a kneeling man.

His clothes had been stripped from him. He was blindfolded, and his hands were tied behind his back.

It was Una who spoke first.

'You like women, don't you, Blue Bonecci? You like pussy too, don't you?'

'Oh yes,' murmured Blue who was obviously under the impression that this orgy had been laid on strictly for his own pleasure, not anyone else's.

'Then kiss it,' Una ordered. 'Come to it on your knees.' She jerked at a leash that was attached to a studded collar around his neck.

On bended knees, Blue headed for her and aimed his

mouth in the general direction of her pussy.

She avoided it. 'Gently,' she ordered. 'Stick out your tongue first. Then and only then, I'll allow you to lick it.'

Flying on wings of sheer lust, Blue obeyed. His tongue stuck out for a moment before its tip connected with her pubic fur.

'Hmm, lovely,' she murmured before grinding her pubes into his face. He struggled for a moment, then gave up as the other two girls held his head tight against Una's undulating pelvis.

'Ooow, that is so nice,' she murmured.

A faint ripple of amusement ran through the audience. If Blue noticed, he gave no sign of it. He was lost in her smell and, judging by the priapic proportions of his penis, his mind was completely taken over by lust.

'Now it's Gloria's turn,' she snapped suddenly as she stepped away.

Blue fell forward, but was brought rudely upright by Una pulling on the leash.

Just as before, Blue licked at Gloria's pussy whilst all three women looked down on him, their faces flushed with happiness.

Kitty was the last to have her pussy licked. Then they gagged him.

'That's good,' she said, 'But look at the effect it's having on him.'

She pointed to his penis.

Una got hold of a cane from somewhere.

'Get down!' she exclaimed, and gave it a sharp whack.

The sound of a muffled yell came from behind Blue's

gag. Only those on the stage saw his jaw clench in fear.

'I think we should bridle this thing,' said Una as she trailed the tip of the whip over his bulging cock.

A murmur of approval ran through the audience.

With a small leather bridle in her hands, Gloria knelt beside Blue. Soon his long, hard penis and his balls were encased in straps of leather. At the very tip of his penis hung a brass ring. Another leash was attached to that. It was Kitty who got hold of this one. She gave it a quick jerk.

'This way!'

Muffled sounds of outrage sounded from behind Blue's gag. But he could not avoid walking forward on his knees. He had to obey, and despite his sudden aversion to what they were doing to him, his penis remained erect.

'Get him up onto the table,' ordered Una and passed her leash, the one that connected with the collar around his neck, to Gloria,

Gloria and Kitty eventually got Blue up the set of steps that led onto the table. On the table they got him on all fours, slid a set of stocks over his head, and fastened his wrists and ankles firmly within the thick straps connected to the table.

He could not possibly move, yet undoubtedly he would have done if he could have seen what was to happen next.

'Grease him for me,' cried Una.

She was doing something in the shadows, fixing some item of clothing or apparatus onto herself.

A smiling Gloria brought a pot of what looked like cold cream to Kitty.

With a devilish look in her eyes, Kitty unscrewed the top,

looked to her audience, then back to the squirming Blue.

By now, he must have known that there were more than the three women with him. The audience was getting excited, and the more they did so, the noisier they became.

Blue shivered then struggled against his restraints as Kitty ran a sliver of cold cream along the crack between his buttocks.

His whole body tensed as she slid a copious amount of the cream into his anus, digging her finger in so he would be more receptive for what was to come.

A roar of approval went up from the audience as Una came out of the shadows.

Placing her hands on her hips, she smiled broadly then wiggled her pelvis. The false prick that stood proud of her body waved around before her.

'Now,' she cried to her audience, 'Let's see if he's as good at receiving what he's so good at giving out.'

The second roar of approval was more noisy than the first.

'Give it to him!' cried a woman from the first row.

'Fuck him!' cried another.

Una raised her arms for silence. 'Do you think he deserves it?'

'Yes!' went up the cry. 'Yes! Yes! Yes!'

'From all three of us?' Una asked.

'*Yes! Yes!*'

Una began to mount the steps. When she got to the one from where she could get at him best, his buttocks began to shudder, and his body twisted wildly.

'Steady,' she said gently, and began to caress his body. 'Steady.'

She nodded at Kitty who began to pull on the leash that was connected to his penis.

'Just to let you know it's still there,' she said, partly to her audience, but also for Blue's benefit.

A sudden hush fell over her audience as she aimed her rubber protrusion at Blue's pulsating anus.

His whole body tensed as the head of it nudged aside a reluctant sphincter. The first inch was in and Una was feeling triumphant. She pushed a little more. A vast cry of delight went up from the audience. The penis she was wearing disappeared completely into the recumbent man.

He tried struggling, but Una knew he could not get away from her.

She could feel the muscles of his buttocks becoming hard as nails as she abused his anus. The delight of having him at her mercy was incredibly arousing. Besides that, the rubber that fixed the phallus to her body was rubbing against her clitoris and causing eruptions of delight. Her time was coming. His wasn't, at least, not yet.

Blue was in her power, and for the first time ever, she knew how a man felt when he was giving it to a woman. There was power there, a superior feeling that it was him who was doing, and her who was being done to.

She knew that behind his gag he would be cursing her. Strangely enough, she had expected him to be able to throw her off by now.

Was this merely her own orgasm she was feeling? Or was she drunk with her feelings of power and revenge?

Surprising sensations swept over her. She tried to control them, suppress them and send them back to where they had come. But her response was as natural as ever. She was having sex with a man. Her nipples were hardening, and that hidden, pulsating button was responding in the same way it had always responded.

In spite of what she was doing, or indeed, because of it, waves of climax seemed to break out of her very pores and roll over her body like a film of fresh sweat.

There was no stopping its progress; no preventing it with the power of her mind. Her mind was no match for what nature intended.

Just as she did when a man put his stem into her, she threw back her head, closed her eyes, and drifted on the currents of sexual climax.

A great cry of applause accompanied by prolonged hand clapping arose from the audience.

'Encore!' went up the cry from one solitary person in the front row, an Italian looking woman with big brown eyes, and a good figure despite her middle age.

'Encore,' went up the echo. The word multiplied until it reached a crescendo.

Una gave the mockery of a bow, the rubber phallus still attached to her waist and still embedded in the man before her.

She gave a quick signal to Kitty. Kitty grinned, and acknowledging the audience, waltzed gracefully across the stage and proceeded to help Una unbuckle the mock phallus from her person.

Kitty stood four square behind Blue. She waved her arms in the air as Una re-buckled the straps. The audience went wild.

Una took hold of the leash that was attached to the harness that imprisoned Blue's penis. Like Kitty had done, she began to pull on it.

This part of the scenario did not take long. Kitty, aroused by watching Una, came very quickly. The audience cheered as they had before. This time it was Gloria's turn.

Blue was strangely quiet. Una checked his gag and although she feared doing it, she dared look into his eyes. What she saw there surprised her. His eyes were still blue. Nothing could change that. But there was a look of realisation in them, a kind of helplessness born of deep shame.

'One more,' she whispered, and touched his cheek. It was hot and looked red.

Gloria made the most of riding the man who had ridden her. Her large, rounded buttocks quivered. She put all her energy into every thrust she gave him and looked to be thoroughly enjoying her task.

'Take that!' she cried. 'And that! And that!'

Again and again she slammed her pelvis against him so that the imitation penis went as far as it could go.

She laughed as she did it, and for a while Una thought she had completely lost her mind.

But she came back, and Una could see by her expression that she too was climaxing.

Once she had completely finished, all three naked women walked to the front of the stage and bowed low.

En masse, their audience rose to their feet, hands clapping. More cries of *Encore* reverberated around the room.

The three women on stage exchanged looks with each other.

'We have to include him,' Una whispered.

'Why? He deserved all he got!' pronounced a bubbling Gloria, earlier nervousness completely forgotten.

'Because he's going to kill us if we don't show his face to the audience.'

Kitty and Gloria looked at each other rather than at her.

'Come on,' ordered Una.

They untied his wrists and took the leather from his neck and his penis. His eyes looked to each of them in turn as he took off his own gag.

It was hard to tell exactly how he was going to react, so all three stepped away from him.

'Encore! Marvellous! More!' shouted the audience.

Their loud shouts grabbed Blue's attention. He looked at them, blinked as if not quite understanding what he was seeing.

But Una was watching. If the look on his face was anything to go by, she had a fair idea of how he was feeling and what he would do next.

She saw his chest swell as he took a deep breath. Then he stepped forward, his head rotating slowly as he sought to identify the sort of people who would enjoy watching what they had just watched.

A look of shock appeared on his face as he realised exactly who his audience were.

'They're all women,' he said in disbelief. 'Dames. They're all dames!'

The three women with him moved quietly away.

'Let's get out of here,' Una whispered. They left Blue to his adoring audience.

* * *

Ice and Johnnie Angel were waiting for them in Johnnie's car.

'Step on it!' shouted Ice once the girls were in.

'What's the rush?' Una asked.

'Are you kidding?' Ice was no longer the cool man of power whose voice cut like a knife through butter. He was frightened, and no one in that car could blame him.

Una grabbed hold of his arm.

'It's OK, Ice, Everything will be just fine.'

He turned to her. She winced as she saw the fear in his eyes.

'That guy would quite happily cut my balls off and make them into castanets.'

'What's castanets?' asked Gloria.

No one answered her. Everyone knew her voice was high-pitched because she was as frightened as they were.

'Bus station or train station?' Johnnie asked.

'Relax.' Una was adamant. 'I saw his face. I saw the look in his eyes. Blue Bonecci is not the man he was. I guarantee it.'

Ice looked at her in disbelief. 'You guarantee it.'

She smiled. 'Sure,' she said. 'Let me tell you a little story.'

'This is no time for stories!' cried Kitty.

'Listen,' Una touched her arm. 'Did you see that little Italian woman sat down the front of the audience tonight?'

Gloria shrugged. Kitty nodded. 'I think so. Why?'

'That was Blue Bonecci's mother. I've met her before. I met her a while ago too. She was out with that daughter of

199

hers, and she was looking upset. I asked her what was wrong. Reluctantly, she told me she wanted to see her son married. She didn't like the way he treated women, and she didn't want it to go on. He needed to be made to feel shame and guilt for his behaviour. He needed to be treated like he treated them. Now, I also knew from the receptionist who works for those doctors on Brown Street that Mrs Bonecci is given special treatment. By that I mean she's a broad-minded lady who thinks men should treat women well, and that women should enjoy the same privileges as men do. So I put her in the picture about our little club and what we intended to do about Blue. I guaranteed he'd be a changed man afterwards.' The others looked at her in disbelief.

'You've got to be joking!' Kitty looked astounded.

'Well, you sure kept that a little secret,' said Ice as he tipped his hat to the back of his head.

'I'd like to think our treatment did him some good,' Gloria remarked. 'I feel almost as though I've changed a sinner into a saint.'

'He's no saint!' So engrossed in their own achievements, they'd all forgotten about the Federal Agent who was driving the car. He pulled in to the side of the road and turned round in his seat. 'That guy is still going down.'

'You can't arrest him!' Gloria's voice sounded as if she were verging on tears.

'But that was our deal. You give me the details of his boot-legging operation up in Canada, and I get him locked up where the nearest thing to a woman is a guy from Brooklyn who wears lipstick and answers to the name of Gloria – begging your pardon, Gloria.'

Una sat back in her seat. 'Then I won't give you the evidence.'

Ice's hand covered hers. 'You have to, Una. That was the deal.'

Una sighed. 'How long will he get?'

Johnnie shrugged. 'Depends who speaks up for him. If an agent says he came quietly and was co-operative, then he could be out in five years, perhaps less.'

'Perhaps less,' echoed Ice, 'Especially seeing as we're talking about boot-legging. Is it true that Prohibition is about to be repealed?'

Johnnie looked uncomfortable. 'Well, it is, but that's no excuse . . .'

'We could make things awkward for you if you don't help him out,' said Kitty.

Now Johnnie really did look awkward.

'You could help, couldn't you?' purred Una.

'Sure you could,' echoed Gloria.

Johnnie looked defeated. There was no way he could cope with three delicious females all working hard on his person to have their own way. They could have their own way any time.

'Alright,' he said at last. 'I'll see what I can do.'

Everyone sighed with relief.

Una turned to Ice. 'We'd better be going.'

'You're going?' asked Johnnie. 'New York?'

They both shook their heads.

'Into another world,' said Una with a smile. 'We're leaving the city to the wolves, and going where the wolves roam free.'

'But what about the club?' asked Gloria.

'Give it back to your benefactor,' said Una. 'I've got no need of it.'

'I'll miss you,' said Kitty and hugged them both.

'So will I,' echoed Gloria.

'Good luck,' Johnnie added.

Una and Ice got out of the car. The remaining occupants watched them go.

'Are they really going back to the wilderness?' Gloria asked.

'Apparently so,' answered Kitty. 'I should imagine you could run about naked up there and no one would ever know.'

'Really?' said a thoughtful Gloria, and thanked her lucky stars that her plans would take her somewhere glamorous enough to suit her name.

Chapter 23

The sun had only just risen over the pine trees, but Ice and Una were already out and on their way down the track.

The lake lay only some two hundred feet below them, its silvery waters gleaming like a mirror in the sunlight.

'Race you there,' she shouted.

Her long brown legs broke into a slow run. He began to run too, but made no real effort to close the gap between them.

How much better, he thought, to view her naked buttocks from behind.

Even now, as he ran, he looked with pleasure on the rolling rhythm of her nut-brown behind, the intricate detail of her spinal column beneath the sun-kissed skin, and the way her jet-black hair caught the light of the sun.

It was long again now, just as it had been when he'd first met her. On that occasion, he had shared her body with his friend Blue Bonecci. He shared her with no one nowadays. Not that they ever saw anyone special that might make eyes at her. But he knew she would not respond. She was like the red deer, she was back in her wilderness and she was happy just being with him.

'Come on,' she called over her shoulder. He laughed and slowed to a walk.

'You go on without me. I can't keep up with you even though you are fat as a barrel.'

She only laughed at his remark. *She knew what I meant*, he thought.

By the time he got to the lake, she was already swimming, her head a tiny black dot among the golden glow of the sun-touched lake.

'Come on in!' she shouted.

He waved and laughed too. He wasted no time. Like her, he was already completely unclothed. He did not wade in through the shallows as she usually did, but flung himself full stretch.

At first the coldness of the water took his breath away. Then he rallied and welcomed its instant freshness.

He swam towards her.

'Go away!' she called and splashed water at him.

'I'm coming!' he cried, and with one last thrust at the water, he was with her, his arms holding her close.

Water dripped from their hair and ran over their faces as they kissed. Their lips parted. Beneath the water, he ran his hand down over her full breasts and her fuller stomach.

'I am fat,' she said, and he knew she was seeking his reassurance.

He kissed her before speaking.

'You are fat,' he replied, 'But I love you. Both of you,' and he patted the growing mound that had once been her flat belly.

Chapter 24

It had never occurred to Kitty to work for the Feds before. An office job, perhaps, but to be asked to do some undercover work that might involve using her very obvious physical talents, was a very different and interesting matter.

'You're a natural, honey,' said Johnnie Angel. Seeing as she rather liked the guy and couldn't get enough of the way he screwed her, she decided to accept the job.

'Will I get fringe benefits?' she asked one night when their clothes were half off and his erection was only partial.

'As long as you remember how and where to use your mouth.' He smiled at her. 'And I bet my bottom dollar that at this moment in time you know exactly where to begin.'

They exchanged knowing looks before Kitty spread her painted finger nails over his chest. From there, she proceeded to lick her way down his body, over his navel, and into the tangle of hair that decorated his lower stomach.

As it turned out, Kitty was very good at her job, probably because it involved everything she liked doing. She liked the undercover work, and she also liked the under the covers work.

In time, she was noticed by the higher administration of

the CIA. Foreign dignitaries, she was told, are not always what they seemed. Some of them were in the country for covert operations – spies in fact. It was her job to gain the confidence, and possibly the bed of such people.

Kitty jumped at the chance. She'd tired of Johnnie Angel and she liked plenty of variety in her job. The Eighteenth Amendment was repealed, and she'd grown tired of mobsters. Foreign diplomats and ambassadors were much more interesting. And such a variety of shapes, sizes and colours.

By the time she retired at the age of thirty-four, Kitty Fitzpatrick could write a book on the people she had met, both in Washington and abroad.

With regard to her having access to such privileged information, she was awarded a pension subject to her signing a contract that categorically stated she would never divulge the boudoir secrets of those in positions of power.

Chapter 25

Gloria had become stage-struck. Well, not exactly stage-struck, but movie-struck.

She ran the Amazon Club for a while before selling it. Conveniently, she omitted giving any of the money back to her benefactor who had provided it in the first place.

But Gloria's mind was on other things. Her ambition lay in another direction, and that was due west.

After the night at the Amazon Club when she had taken her turn with her sisters in arms at shaming the hedonistic Blue Bonecci, the memory of all that applause stayed with her.

Night after night, whether she was alone or with a lover, the music of that night, the clapping and the calls for more, reverberated around in her mind.

In her mind there was no one else on the stage when all that acclaim was pronounced. There was only her, the prettiest, the most vivacious person in the whole room, and in fact, the whole city.

Pictures of Mary Pickford and Paulette Goddard decorated the walls of her kitchen, and sometimes she would sigh and tell them they'd be jealous when she got to Hollywood.

And she didn't take long about it. There was nothing to keep her in Chicago. No job and no man she cared for as much as she had Blue Bonecci.

She packed herself just one case of best clothes. Movie stars never wore cast-offs or items that were severely out of style. So she wouldn't do that, because, after all, she was intending to be a movie star.

'You a movie star? You and thousands of others,' Kitty had told her.

Gloria had ignored her. Pouting her lips, her big bottom wiggling provocatively from side to side, she set out in search of her dream.

In fact, Gloria was a lot more successful than either Kitty or people in general had anticipated.

On arrival in Hollywood, she took up with a Jewish banker who had just lost his wife. The wife had been older and wealthier than him, so he found himself the inheritor of many millions of dollars. He also found himself with a lot of time on his hands, and a huge house painted cream and built in a hacienda style.

Being an older man and his wife having become nothing more than a companion in latter years, both the man, his libido and his money were ready for someone like Gloria. In no time at all she was his wife and a budding starlet after having persuaded him to invest some money in the film industry.

Gloria made the ideal starlet. She was brash, blonde and beautiful, and perfectly chaperoned by an older man whose money was the anchor that kept her body firmly close to his.

When people asked how she had got started in the

business, she told them she got her first break playing a lead role in *Love's Labours Lost* by William Shakespeare.

She'd never seen the play in her life, and never knew the story. She'd just picked up a book in her husband's vast private library. She had heard of William Shakespeare, and although her husband had many copies of his work, it was this particular title that she liked, but had never read.

Chapter 26

Rosa Bonecci got her way.

Something unique had happened to her son, Blue Bonecci, on that night at the Amazon nightclub.

It wasn't so much that he had seen the error of his ways, but his ego had been reduced in size, and so, as it turned out, had his penis.

Strong-minded women, with some idea of what they wanted and where they were going, now had no room in his life.

Of course, he still carried on the family business of breaking the law in pursuit of making money, but he was less sociable than he had been.

Rosa spoke to Father O'Flanagan about him.

'He's changed,' she told him brightly. 'He's a different man. So much more responsible. So much more considerate for his family's feelings.'

Sean O'Flanagan cleared his throat before he spoke. 'Do you think that God had something to do with it?'

Rosa smiled and shook her head. 'Father, if I told you that I've taken to frequenting nightclubs, would you be shocked?'

211

His jaw dropped slightly, but she admired the way he recovered.

'I must admit to some surprise. What was your purpose in frequenting such places?'

She looked away. Her eyes followed the fleeting shadows she saw go by out in the street on the other side of the stained glass windows.

'I wanted to live, Father. I wanted to feel again all the sensations I experienced in my youth. After watching the most incredible cabaret I have ever seen in my life, I suddenly realised that my son's wayward ways were about to end.' She turned her face back to him, saw him colour slightly, and knew immediately what was in his head. 'I came here today to give thanks, Sean. I also came here because I wanted to say that I forgive you.'

His eyes became very round as he stared at her.

'For-forgive me?' The words almost choked him. He shook his head, raised his hand to his brow which glistened with sweat. 'Yes, Maria. I see what you mean . . .'

'No,' she interrupted gently, 'Not for Maria. There is nothing to forgive. I love my daughter. Her father, the man whose name appears on the birth certificate, he loves her too. It is not that for which I forgive you. I forgive you for fearing to love me, for looking at me with those bright blue eyes of yours and dreaming of me alone in your great big wooden bed. I forgive you for not opening your heart and claiming me as your own.'

He blinked at her like an owl just woken from its sleep.

'I realise now that you are not a brave man, though a sensitive one. So I forgive you for that too.'

'Rosa, what can I say . . . What can I do?'

She reached out and touched his arm, caressing the dark cloth of his jacket with her thumb.

Her look was intensely beautiful.

'You can do something for me. We no longer have any close relatives back in the old country. Can you write to a country priest of your choice and ask him if there are any old fashioned virgins there who would suit my son's new character?'

Chapter 27

At first, Blue was afraid to even meet the little girl from Naples who had been chosen to be his wife. And she wasn't much more than a little girl. She was barely sixteen.

'She will suit you fine,' his mother told him in the presence of their parish priest. She leaned a little closer and spoke to him in a whisper. 'She knows nothing of men. You will have to go gently with her. Apart from that, she speaks no English. Your reputation will be safe.'

Like some others he knew, mostly from his father's generation, Blue Bonecci married a quiet country girl who spent most of her early years in the States staring down at her shoes, too timid to look him straight in the eyes.

In time, his ego was restored. So was the size of his dick.

But the three women he had let down in his past had left him with a severe case of fidelity. No more would he seduce any woman who looked fair game. The possibility of being shamed again, like Una and her friends had shamed him, was too awful to contemplate.

Tony, his younger brother, also became a more subdued man than he had been. As with everything in their lives, the younger brother followed the example of the older one. He

215

got married, and made Rosa his mother very happy.

Only one other beside Rosa knew Blue's secret. She had watched, intrigued and excited by what she was seeing. Unknown to her mother, Maria had followed Rosa to the Amazon Club on that incredible night, and the memory was implanted in her brain.

Much to her parents' surprise, Maria Bonecci grew up to be an exotic dancer, a dream she had held dear following a certain night at a certain club when her brother had learned a terrible lesson.